Esca

The perfect destin
can they make it a lifetime?

In the heart of Provence, the picturesque Fontesquieu vineyard is famous for its wines...and for the gorgeous billionaire bachelors who run it!

Amid the rolling hills and exquisite views of the glittering Mediterranean, Dominic and Raoul Fontesquieu are determined to continue their family's enduring legacy. But when two women arrive at the vineyard, the vines aren't the only things to flourish in the summer sun...

Discover Dominic's story in
Falling for Her French Tycoon

And Raoul's story in
Falling for His Unlikely Cinderella

Both available now!

Dear Reader,

Over the last few years, one of my favorite television series has been *Downton Abbey*. When I was watching Daisy, the kitchen maid, hurriedly preparing the kindling for a fire in the massive library and making a botch of it, I was reminded of the original story of Cinderella.

Poor Cinderella had been highborn, but she had been relegated to cleaning cinders out of the fireplace. It's a timeless story, rewritten over and over again throughout the years because we all love to root for her to overcome the barriers and be with the prince she adores. We also cheer for the prince, who must choose a princess to marry, but we know Cinderella is his heart's desire. Will they gain their eventual happiness?

Our delight in reading a Cinderella story again and again is to see how the two ill-fated lovers finally get together. None of us tire of reading another version of the original time-honored story called *Cendrillon*, written by the Frenchman Charles Perrault.

My novel, a version of *Cinderella*, has been set in my favorite location of Provence, France. I've loved writing about two wonderful people who deserve each other despite the outer and inner forces keeping them apart.

Enjoy!

Rebecca Winters

Falling for His Unlikely Cinderella

Rebecca Winters

Recycling programs for this product may not exist in your area.

ISBN-13: 978-1-335-55626-4

Falling for His Unlikely Cinderella

This edition published by arrangement with Harlequin Books S.A.

For questions and comments about the quality of this book, please contact us at CustomerService@Harlequin.com.

Harlequin Enterprises ULC
22 Adelaide St. West, 40th Floor
Toronto, Ontario M5H 4E3, Canada
www.Harlequin.com

Printed in U.S.A.

Rebecca Winters lives in Salt Lake City, Utah. With canyons and high alpine meadows full of wildflowers, she never runs out of places to explore. They, plus her favorite vacation spots in Europe, often end up as backgrounds for her romance novels—because writing is her passion, along with her family and church. Rebecca loves to hear from readers. If you wish to email her, please visit her website at rebeccawinters.net.

Books by Rebecca Winters

Harlequin Romance

Escape to Provence

Falling for Her French Tycoon

The Princess Brides

The Princess's New Year Wedding
The Prince's Forbidden Bride
How to Propose to a Princess

Holiday with a Billionaire

Captivated by the Brooding Billionaire
Falling for the Venetian Billionaire
Wedding the Greek Billionaire

The Magnate's Holiday Proposal

Visit the Author Profile page
at Harlequin.com for more titles.

To my darling, devoted Rachel, who's a dear friend and a saint besides being a spectacular wife and mother to three adorable children. Over the years, we've talked about everything under the sun. As you can guess, the poor thing has had to put up with me telling her about my ideas for new novels. With her expertise as a voracious reader, marathon runner, nurse and carpenter, she has supplied marvelous suggestions that have helped me develop characters in my books. *What would I do without you, Rachel?*

Praise for
Rebecca Winters

"There are tender moments, bouts of excitement and, of course, raw emotion. A delectable read that readers won't want to end!"

—*Goodreads* on *Whisked Away by Her Sicilian Boss*

CHAPTER ONE

Monday, December 1

IN A STATE of euphoria, Raoul Fontesquieu left the apartment at the Château Fontesquieu in Vence, France, and headed for his office. He was now officially on vacation from work. Once he'd gathered up a few things and had talked to his cousin Dominic, he had big plans. But on the way, he heard his cell ring. It was only six in the morning!

A grimace marred his features when he saw his father's name on the caller ID before picking up. *"Qu'est ce qui se passe?"*

"I'm calling from the Sacred Heart. Your *gran'pere* was transported to the hospital a few minutes ago. He's in room 407 and isn't expected to live past the next hour. We expect you here *now*!"

Matthieu Fontesquieu, Raoul's intransigent father, didn't know how to do anything but demand obedience. Being his parents' only child, he'd borne the emotional scars of such treatment for as long as he could remember.

Over the last week the family had sensed this day was coming. Armand Fontesquieu, the eighty-five year-old, impossibly autocratic CEO of the Domaine Fontesquieu in Provence-Alpes-Côte d'Azur, was drawing his last breath.

News of his death would ring throughout Provence and the wine world, but Raoul wouldn't mourn him. As a little boy he'd tried once to establish a relationship with him, but had been shot down and had never tried again.

"I'll be there as soon as I can."

Once he'd hung up, Raoul turned his car around and drove out of the Fontesquieu estate for the hospital. Upon reaching it, he took the elevator to the fourth floor and strode down the hall. His mother and father had been watching for him. She seemed particularly anxious, which was not a good sign. Something was up. He just didn't know what.

"Your *gran'pere* is waiting for you," his father murmured.

Waiting? While he was on the verge of death?

Raoul frowned, looking around for Dominic. Neither he nor his dozen other cousins were here. "What's going on?"

"You'll understand in a minute. Let's go in."

Raoul entered the hospital room filled with his aunts and uncles and saw his grandfather lying in the bed hooked up to IVs and oxygen.

His father nudged him. "Tell him you've arrived."

He was sick of his father's orders, but now wasn't the time to defy him. He walked over to the bed. "Gran'pere? It's Raoul. I'm here."

The old man didn't open his eyes. How sad that even now, Raoul couldn't conjure any feelings for someone so cold.

"Raoul?" He spoke in a loud enough voice to reach everyone. "I want the family to hear from my own lips that *you* are now the CEO of the Fontesquieu Domaine." In another minute his grandfather, plagued by liver disease, exhaled and was gone.

His father took hold of his arm. "The family has arrangements to make," he whispered. "Stay available. We'll talk later today about your new position and get you installed."

He sucked in his breath. The last position Raoul would ever want would be CEO of the Fontesquieu family wine business. He was already busy with plans for a future that had nothing to do with the family.

Before dying, that grasping excuse for a human being had colluded with his favorite son Matthieu to put Raoul in charge for one reason only. By making him the CEO, it was their last bribe to bend Raoul to their will.

They assumed this grand gesture would force him to call off his divorce to Sabine Murat. Both families had been fighting it to preserve all the Murat millions with the Fontesquieu fortune. Both fortunes together enabled the families to continue to buy more assets.

But no coup could have accomplished

what they'd hoped for. Raoul had never loved Sabine. Now it was over and finished, *grace à Dieu*. His divorce from Sabine Murat had been finalized yesterday afternoon. That was all he'd been waiting for.

This morning Raoul was free to embrace his new life with his precious eighteen-month-old son.

Overjoyed that Alain's existence no longer had to be kept a secret from the world, Raoul left the hospital for the modern Fontesquieu office building where all the family head offices were housed, including his own as president of marketing and sales. It was located behind the immense seventeenth-century château on the estate of the famous Fontesquieu vineyards drawing tourists from around the world.

He phoned Dominic. They were closer than brothers. It was Dominic who'd insisted Raoul stay with him in his suite at the château throughout his two months' separation from Sabine. During that period Dominic had gotten married and moved out for good. Now it was Raoul's turn to leave the château and never come back. This morning he had so much to tell Dominic, he was going to explode if they couldn't talk right now.

To his relief, Dominic, the funds manager for the Fontesquieu corporation, had opened the door of his own office suite to wait for him. "Come on in. I only heard the news about our grandfather a little while ago. It seems wrong not to mourn him, but I don't have those feelings."

"Tell me about it," Raoul muttered. "I got the call at six. Papa ordered me to get to the hospital. I arrived just in time for our grandfather to announce to the room that *I* was the new CEO before he took his last breath. You and I both know the reason why."

Grim faced, his cousin nodded. "Even with death approaching, they planned it down to the last minute."

"He and Papa don't give up, but as you know, I would never have taken over, and before long I'll be leaving the family business. The good news is, last night I got a call from my attorney Horace. The divorce decree was granted yesterday at the end of the day. I would have called you, but the news came too late to disturb you. Dom—I'm a free man and can live like one!"

"Raoul—" Dominic hugged him so hard he almost knocked him over.

"It wiped out a good portion of my assets, but it was worth it."

"If you need help, I'm your man."

"I know that and am grateful, but my new business is growing and I'm already recouping. Papa said he'd call me later in order to install me, but I have news for him. When he phones, I'll refuse to accept it and wish him luck in his new position—the one he's always coveted. Now he can be both comptroller and CEO."

Dominic nodded. "We might have my father, three uncles and two aunts, all Fontesquieux, who are more than capable of taking over Grandfather's empire, but you and I both know *your* father is the one who'll run everything now. He's made in the old man's hard-boiled image with my father a clone of both of them."

Raoul stared at him. "Good luck to him. Little does he know I'm resigning soon. Already I've gathered new clients for the company I've started. Over the last two months the list has been growing."

"You're a genius."

"Great Uncle Jerome was the genius who gave me the idea before he died."

"Nevertheless, I can't imagine the company without you."

"I've been wanting to leave for years."

"What do you mean?"

"I was bound by a secret and couldn't tell you the real reason why I didn't join you in Paris. But with Grandfather's death, I no longer have to stay silent. The truth is, I would have joined you in Paris when I turned eighteen, but by then Jerome was diagnosed with lung cancer."

"You're kidding—"

Raoul shook his head. "He swore me to secrecy and didn't even tell Danie. You know what he was like. Because he was a scientist, he handled his health care in his own way and turned to alternative medicine."

"How did he do it exactly?"

"He used holistic interventions of supplements, herbs, enzymes, plus he changed his diet and he prayed. Knowing he would eventually die, I couldn't leave him because I loved him too much. But it was hard not being able to tell you the truth at the time."

"I understand totally. Gran'pere Armand never liked or acknowledged him, but Jerome had you and loved you like the son he could never have." Dominic eyed him solemnly. "What's so sad is that your father has to know he lost you years ago."

"Amen," Raoul ground out. "Before the day is out everyone will have heard about the divorce being granted, but that's irrelevant. Right now, I've got to see about getting my villa furnished, starting with the nursery. Alain needs a crib. Want to come with me for a couple of hours?"

"What do you think?" an elated Dominic cried. "I'm all yours for now." He gave some instructions to his assistant Theo, then turned to Raoul. "Let's go!" They left the building and climbed into Raoul's Jaguar.

At 8:00 a.m., twenty-six-year-old Camille Delon, known to her friends as Cami, packed a lunch for her and her mother.

Together they left their apartment on the main floor of the eight-plex located in the lower income area of Vence, France. They walked toward the van parked around the side with the company logo, Nettoyage Internationale.

A chilly breeze would have blown Cami's shoulder-length black hair around if she hadn't formed it into a chignon. Her blue pullover sweater felt good over her T-shirt and jeans as she got behind the wheel. From the time she'd started working with her mother seven years ago, they'd agreed Cami should do the bulk of the driving since her mom didn't feel that comfortable maneuvering the van in heavy traffic.

She closed the door and drove them to the housecleaning office in the heart of Vence to get their next assignment. NI, a premier housecleaning and housekeeping service, had offices all over Provence and were great employers.

"Bonjour!" the manager, Helene Biel, greeted them when they walked inside her office. Three other full-time coworkers, Jeanne, Marise and Patrice, who usually worked together, had come in another company van and were already assembled.

"Now that you're all here, I'm sending the five of you out on a lengthy assignment. The new owner of a property with a large, ultra-exclusive villa needs a total housecleaning: walls, ceilings, woodwork, windows, thorough scrubbing of kitchen and bathrooms, main rooms, fixtures, vents, floors, fireplaces, patio, you name it. The only room you're not to touch is the study on the main floor, which will be locked.

"He wants it spotless before he can start furnishing the place. After visiting the site, I estimate it will take you ladies four to five days. I'll let them know you're on your way now. That's it. This is the address."

After hearing its location, Cami eyed her mother wordlessly. This villa was located in the most elite, prestigious area of Vence. Only billionaires could afford to live on the top ridge of hills that overlooked the whole spectacular landscape stretching to the Mediterranean.

With an address like that, it had to be near her favorite fairy-tale-like Château Fontesquieu, one of the wonders of Provence, set in the middle of its world-famous vineyards. The thought brought incredibly happy memories associated with her father. When Cami had been little, her dad, who'd been a taxi driver before his fatal car crash, had driven her and her mom to the estate every fall to see it and she'd never forgotten.

She must have been five years old when he'd first taken them on a tour through the vineyards at harvest time so they could watch the workers picking the grapes. Every year after that during the harvest he did the same thing, stopping each time for them to take in the sights.

One particular incident stood out in her mind and had always lingered there. At the age of twelve, she'd seen an older man walking through the vineyard with a young dark-haired man, maybe fifteen or sixteen. He was so handsome, she'd put down the back window so she could lean out and look at him a little better. They appeared to be supervising the workers before they reached the man's elegant black car with the gold hood ornament. As the younger man turned to get in, he caught Cami staring at him and smiled.

A thrill ran through her young girl's heart and she smiled back before the other car drove off. When she asked her father about the ornament, he said it was the emblem of the royal Fontesquieu family, which had existed for hundreds of years.

Cami sat back. In her mind's eye the younger man had to be one of the royals, the fictional prince who lived at the château. Nothing could have delighted her more and caused her to dream about living in there with him one day as his princess.

But in November of that very year her father had been killed. The pain and shock of losing him stripped her of such a foolish fantasy. No more trips to the vineyard or anything else. By the time she'd turned twenty-one with a brief, failed marriage behind her, she'd been forced to face another personal crisis.

Her doctor had said that in time the genetic heart murmur she'd been born with would have to work too hard. He explained to her that she had a bicuspid aortic valve. The surgeon ran tests and decided to put off surgery until the symptoms began to affect her life, possibly when she turned twenty-six. By then the technique would have been perfected and become less invasive, possibly avoiding open-heart surgery altogether.

She was allowed to do her normal work, but there could be no running marathons or doing any physical activity that raised her heartbeat to too high a level. To make certain she was taking care of herself, she had to go in for regular checkups. The doctor said she could continue to clean houses, but to do no heavy lifting.

This last October the doctor scheduled her operation for mid-December. The heart surgeon had plans to leave the country over the holidays, so the operation had to be done before that time.

There were no guarantees where her recovery was concerned. As the time grew near, Cami had to live with that prospect, even though the doctor sounded reasonably optimistic. But the alternative of not undergoing the surgery meant her days would be numbered.

Except for their extended family in Nice,

Cami and her mother had never told anyone that she had to have an operation, not even Helene or their coworkers. She was lucky to have this job and needed it too much to lose it. At her last doctor's appointment, they had set the date of the operation for December 18, giving her the holidays to recover.

But what if she didn't?

As the doctor had told her, every surgery held a risk. In order not to dwell on it, Cami worked harder than ever and determined to make the most of her life—until she couldn't.

"You're to park in front and go to the front door," Helene explained. "Call me if there's any problem. Now off you go."

Since they had all the equipment they needed in their vans, they filed outside under a semicloudy sky. Cami got in the van with her mother and they started driving toward the verdant hills in the distance. The other van followed them. Slowly they wound their way serpentine style to the summit. How would it be to live up here in this glorious paradise?

As they passed by the entrance to the

Fontesquieu estate and vast vineyards open for tourists, she eyed the impressive grilled gate with its gold ducal crest. Her mother noticed it too. "You probably don't remember what your father said the last time he drove us around there years ago."

"No, but I do remember all the times Papa took us there." Passing by here reminded her of that special day when the handsome young man had smiled at her. "Tell me what he said." She'd loved her dad and had suffered after he'd died.

"The Fontesquieu family lives at the footsteps of the gods." Her mother shook her head. "I can't comprehend their kind of wealth and never want to. All that money doesn't bring happiness."

"Probably not," Cami murmured. At least that's what you told yourself when you didn't have it. Her wonderful mother had worked so hard all her life, turning to housecleaning after high school to make a living. She'd never stopped.

Cami had just graduated from Sophie Antipolis University in Nice with honors in business and finance. If all went well with the operation and recovery, she'd start work in January at La Maison de Chocolat Gaillard in their finance department where she'd interned during her last semester.

Guaranteed an excellent starting salary, she was determined to pay back the small balance left on her student loan and take care of herself and her mom. No more housecleaning for either of them! Of course, that all depended on the outcome of the operation.

After several turns, they finally reached their destination. The rose-colored two-story villa appearing through the lush greenery was so beautiful, it didn't look real. Several sections of steps rose up the terraced landscaping to the main entry.

Cami pulled the van to a stop in front, thinking that the family who would live in this villa shared those same footsteps her father had once talked about. Feeling as if she'd arrived in a wonderland, Cami got out and started up the stairs with her mother. Before she had a chance to knock, the door opened.

An attractive blonde woman, probably a little older than Cami's mother, smiled at them. “You must be from Nettoyage International.”

Her mother spoke first. “I’m Juliette Delon. This is my daughter, Camille.” Patrice introduced the others.

“Wonderful. I’m Arlette Gilbert. Thank you for being so prompt. Please come inside.”

Cami and her mother followed the woman into the foyer with its fabulous parquet flooring. A graceful winding staircase divided a salon on the right, empty of furnishings, and the sitting room on the left. The interior contained only two chairs and a modern-looking couch. Both rooms were set off with elegant wood carved French doors.

“Won’t you be seated?”

Cami sat on a chair next to her mother. The other three sat on the couch.

The blonde woman studied them. “The owner will be in and out. In the meantime he’s put me in charge and I’ll be here all week. I assume your manager has explained what needs to be done. I’ll take you on a quick tour of the villa and let you decide how to divide up your workload.

"After the tour, I suggest you drive your vans up the driveway where you can park in the rear between the garage and the outdoor swimming pool. I'll unlock the back door so you can bring in your equipment. If you need me, you'll find me here in the sitting room."

Within a half hour they'd moved their vans in back and had made decisions of what areas to tackle first. Cami and her mother chose to clean the four bedrooms with en suite bathrooms upstairs, estimating it would take them several days. All five of them agreed to save washing the windows inside and out until their last day.

They carried their cleaning supplies upstairs. As far as Cami was concerned, this villa was a small palace. What would it be like to live here, to wake up every day to such luxury and beauty, to be able to decorate it the way you wanted and not count the cost?

Her mother shook her head as she looked around. "Just the upkeep on this place would cost a king's ransom. I'm glad it's someone else's headache."

No one could bring Cami down from

the clouds faster than her practical mother. With a resigned smile, she noted that the villa had higher than normal ceilings. The owner had provided a substantial ladder. Being up high made it easy to clean with no extra stress on her heart.

Because Cami's mother had arthritis in her shoulders, Cami insisted on cleaning those, plus the walls and moldings. That left her mom to do the hardwood floors and bathrooms. Their system worked and they got busy.

At noon they walked out to the van to eat their lunch like they always did on the job. Her mother turned on the news. They both liked to know what was going on. The radio would do when there was no TV.

After listening to the world headlines, they heard the announcement that France had lost one of the great vintners from Provence.

"Today France is in mourning over the death of le Duc Armand Fontesquieu, who will be laid to rest on Thursday on the Fontesquieu estate in Vence."

Cami and her mother eyed each other in surprise. They'd passed the famous estate on their way here earlier this morning. What a coincidence!

"The renowned CEO and vintner died at eighty-five years of age and left a dynasty of billions to his family. The future now lies in the hands of his grandson Raoul Fontesquieu, married to Sabine Murat of the Murat industrial millions. Today it was announced he is the new CEO of the Fontesquieu empire. The grandson—"

Her mother turned it off. "I've heard enough."

Cami understood what was going on in her mom's mind. The news was a reminder that 99 percent of the population couldn't relate to a world like the Fontesquieux or billionaires like the owner of the villa they'd been cleaning.

"Let's go in and get started again."

After grabbing lunch, Raoul had driven Dominic back to the office. He turned to his cousin. "Thanks for coming with me this morning. Only you could know how happy I am to be done with the secrecy about Alain. I've almost gone out of my mind having to keep all knowledge of him quiet leading up to the divorce."

"Despite all the problems, you've carried it off."

"But he won't be a secret any longer. As you know, the psychiatrist advised me that Sabine was fragile after losing the baby. No heart trouble had run in her family or mine. It was devastating. That's why I didn't want her to hear of Alain's existence until the divorce was finalized."

Dominic looked at him. "You were fragile too, even though little Celine turned out to be some other man's daughter."

"Nevertheless I loved that baby, but it's all behind me now."

"Nothing could make me happier for you, Raoul."

"My son is going to find out what it's like to have a father who loves him and is free to give him all the attention he needs. If you and Nathalie would get busy, maybe he'll have another little cousin to play with soon."

Dominic grinned. "Who says we haven't been doing our best?"

A chuckle came out of Raoul who felt

a new happiness envelop him. Dominic's wife, Nathalie, had been the one who'd united Raoul with the son he hadn't known anything about. She and Alain's mother, Antoinette, had been stepsisters.

When Antoinette had died of a staph infection ten days after he'd been born, it was Nathalie and her mother who'd looked after Alain in La Gaude, a town fifteen minutes from Vence. But it wasn't until this year's grape harvest that she'd come to the vineyard looking for the nameless father of her nephew. By a miracle she'd found Raoul!

"I'm on vacation from the office for two weeks now. When everything's ready, I'll resign and bring Alain home to the villa. The housecleaning service I engaged on Saturday should be busy there cleaning by now. Arlette volunteered to be in charge."

"Where's Alain?"

"Minerve is tending him during the day while we get the villa ready. By the time the cleaners are through at the end of the week, I'll be leaving your old suite for good."

"Don't worry. We've moved out permanently. Nathalie and I have our own home we're in the process of furnishing. There's no hurry."

"Oh, yes there is. I want nothing more to do with life at the château. Thank heaven for Minerve who's been Alain's nanny since he was born. She's going to come with Arlette to help me with him during the transition. When Alain and I are on our own, I don't want him to miss them too much."

"It'll all work, and Nathalie will help too, but Minerve will be difficult to replace."

"You can say that again. I'm working with an established nanny training service. On Wednesday some women will be sent out for interviews. Arlette will help me vet them."

"She's the perfect one to help. I've got some good news too, Raoul. Arlette couldn't be a better mother-in-law to me and has hired another pharmacist so Nathalie only has to work part-time or not at all. From now on she can help you more when you need it."

"That's terrific."

"Who's going to run the marketing while you're on vacation?"

"I've been grooming our cousin Jean-Pierre to take over for good. He's effective without being pushy. Naturally Papa doesn't approve, but once I've left, Jean-Pierre will be there to save the day. I have great faith in him."

Another smile broke out on Dominic's face. "Then that settles it. Jean-Pierre is the right choice."

They said goodbye and Raoul drove to the villa, eager to take another look at the size of the room he planned to turn into the nursery. He wanted to paint it and needed to estimate how much to buy.

Full of excitement, he entered the villa and bounded up the stairs, but stopped short of entering the room because his breath had caught. An absolutely beautiful woman with a stunning figure was up on the ladder cleaning. She was probably in her midtwenties and totally engaged in her work.

He couldn't remember the last time any woman had caused him to forget what he was doing or thinking for a minute. Not since Antoinette… The same thing had happened with her. He'd taken one look and was so drawn to her, he'd approached her as if in a trance.

Now here he was again three years later, captured by the sight of this stranger. It threw him. He leaned against the doorjamb for a moment before entering.

CHAPTER TWO

AFTER LUNCH, CAMI was back to the second bedroom down the hall from the curved staircase. With her safety glasses on, plus her rubber gloves, she'd climbed the ladder she and her mom had placed on top of the drop cloth.

First, she'd removed the light fixture in the center of the room in order to clean it. Then she vacuumed the cobwebs off the ceiling and cove moldings before scrubbing everything.

As she started to climb down to wash out her flat board mop, she caught sight of a tall, black-haired male lounging against the doorjamb at the entrance. It surprised her so much it caused her to stumble. "Oh—" she cried.

Like lightning he sprang forward on those long powerful legs and saved her from landing on the hardwood floor with a bang, like the mop. "I'm sorry to have startled you," he said in a deep voice, lowering her carefully. She felt his warm breath on her skin.

"It was my fault. Thank you." She stepped back, marveling at his speed and embarrassed to have been that clumsy in front of him.

"I should have knocked on the bedroom door to let you know I was standing there."

She took in the sight of this man who was probably twenty-nine or thirty, dressed in a black cashmere sweater and gray trousers. With those alive black eyes, he was so incredibly attractive, Cami struggled to gain her composure.

"I was deep in thought and probably wouldn't have heard it. Madame Gilbert mentioned the owner would be in and out."

He nodded. "I had something else on my mind too. This room is going to be my son's. I was trying to think what color to paint it tomorrow."

All the bedrooms had off-white walls with white moldings. "How old is he?"

She was still trying to recover. The faint tang of the soap he used in the shower lingered.

"Alain is eighteen months."

A father with a toddler. She wondered if he resembled his gorgeous papa. "Then you must be planning to turn this room into a nursery."

"I was at a furniture store earlier picking out everything and fell in love with a white crib and dresser."

That made her smile. "Is he into trucks or cars?"

A light entered his eyes. "Both. And boats."

While Cami chuckled, trying not to study his striking masculine features through her safety glasses, Madame Gilbert appeared in the doorway.

"Raoul, the gardener is downstairs waiting to talk to you."

"Tell him I'll be right there."

After she disappeared, he plucked the mop off the floor and handed it to Cami. Their hands brushed, causing an unbidden current of electricity to dart through her body. She could still feel the imprint of his hands on her arms. "Forgive me for interrupting your work."

She shook her head. "Thank you for saving me from a crash. All I need is a broken leg."

"Heaven forbid," he murmured. This close he was so handsome it hurt. She'd heard that expression before, but for the first time in her life she felt the truth of it. "It was the least I could do after all your hard work. I can see differences already. We'll definitely be seeing each other again tomorrow," he said with a smile that made her legs go weak before leaving the bedroom.

Long after he'd gone, his smile stayed with her. Something about it haunted her, as if she'd seen it before. Her heart kept thudding. She'd forgotten it could do that.

Struggling to rein in her thoughts, she worked harder than ever, but couldn't forget what had happened. When she'd finished everything and had cleaned up, she carried her equipment to the third bedroom and spread the drop cloth on the floor in preparation for the next day. She put her safety glasses in her purse.

After pulling on her sweater, she walked to the master bedroom to collect her slender, brunette mother who was cleaning the bathroom's exquisite Provençal floor tiles. "How's it going, Maman?"

"How it always goes," came the typical response, then a wry laugh escaped. "I'll be ready to leave in a minute."

"No hurry." Cami looked around. It made total sense that the owner's bedroom was next to the nursery. She wondered why his wife hadn't been here to let them in this morning. But anything to do with him was none of her business. Cami needed to put a governor on her thoughts.

Unfortunately his image remained in her mind and she had difficulty taking her own advice while she helped carry her mom's equipment to the third bathroom so they could begin first thing in the morning. Her mother deserved an easier life. Cami was determined to make that happen for both of them. But the operation might not fix what was wrong. That was the big imponderable.

Soon her mom had finished and their day's work was done, but they'd be back tomorrow. That meant Cami would be seeing *him* again. Her heart did a little kick she seemed to have no control over. Ridiculous when the man had a family, even if she hadn't seen a wedding band.

His fabulous villa had to be worth millions. Though it had sat idle for a while and truly did need a good cleaning, everything looked in excellent condition.

Again she tried to imagine owning a home like his, the kind you'd see in one of the posh interior design magazines from Provence. Imagine living in it with the right man, making a home with him, never worrying that your heart might give out just when life was getting wonderful…

But that was pure fiction. If she wanted any kind of a future for herself and her mother, she would have to work by the sweat of her brow for as long as life and her heart allowed her to draw breath. She had learned never to depend on anyone else.

They asked Madame Gilbert to make sure the ladder was moved to the third bedroom with the drop cloth, then they left. On their way home, she pulled in to their favorite deli to pick up dinner so they wouldn't have to cook. After coming back out, she started up the van and soon she'd parked at the side of their apartment. "We worked hard today. Let's go in. I'm hungry too, Maman."

After walking around the property with the gardener while they discussed what needed to be done, Raoul had gone to the kitchen for a soda. From the window he'd happened to see the housecleaners leave and couldn't help focusing his gaze on the sensational-looking woman who climbed in the driver's seat of the first van.

When he'd started down the upstairs hall earlier in the day, he'd seen her up on the ladder. She had to be five seven, possessing a shapely figure. For a brief moment he'd caught her against his body to prevent her from hitting the floor. Even now he still remembered how she'd felt and the scent of her flowery fragrance.

With her glistening black hair pulled away from her face wearing those safety glasses, she cut a picture that refused to leave his mind. In all his experience he'd never met a female with eyes the exact hue of the tassel hyacinths that grew on Fontesquieu property near the vineyards.

Her coloring was a marvel of nature like Provence itself. It shocked him that he'd become so physically aware of this female when Antoinette's memory had filled his heart for close to three years.

That woman had been the love of his life, but before he could marry her, Sabine Murat, the woman he'd broken up with a month before meeting Antoinette, had come back into his life. He'd slept with Sabine once, but realized he didn't love her. To his shock, Sabine had been to the doctor and was pregnant with Raoul's baby.

His world fell apart. He did the honorable thing by giving up Antoinette and marrying Sabine, but he'd lost the woman he'd loved and concentrated on the coming baby, only to learn after its birth that the baby *wasn't* his and had died of a bad heart within the first month of life.

Sabine had lied to him about the baby's paternity. The news meant he'd been forced to endure needless pain during a soulless marriage, and he divorced her.

He had only recently learned through

Antoinette's stepsister Nathalie that she'd given birth to Raoul's son whom she'd named Alain. Now his life had turned to joy so he could start a new life with his boy. Raoul couldn't wait for everything to be done and left for La Gaude.

Arlette, Alain's grandmother, had already gone home in her car. En route he dropped by his former suite in the north wing of the Château Fontesquieu where Sabine had remained during the separation. There were two averaged-sized framed oil paintings of significance to him, plus a set of two journals he wanted bequeathed to him by his great uncle Jerome. They represented the life work of a master vintner.

It didn't surprise him to see that before Sabine had returned to her parents' château in nearby St. Paul-de-Vence, she'd literally cleaned everything out, including those items she knew he valued most. He grimaced as he looked around. Somehow he'd find a way to get them back. As for right now, he had the satisfaction of knowing the whole ghastly ordeal had come to an end.

Raoul tossed his key on the kitchen

counter and closed the door literally on his old life before walking back out to his car. Being with his son had made him feel reborn. He left the estate, eager to be with Alain.

Tomorrow the man who'd serviced the swimming pools for the former owner would be coming to the villa to check out the indoor pool and get it ready. The outdoor pool had a cover over it. He'd worry about it in the spring.

Now was the time to teach Alain how to swim. Raoul planned that he and his son would get use out of it every day. In time they'd be going out on the Mediterranean in his sailboat. It was vital his boy be able to handle himself in any kind of water.

When he thought about tomorrow, the knowledge that the cleaning people would be at the villa for a few more days was an added plus. He intended to find out the gorgeous woman's name and more.

By 8:00 a.m. Tuesday, Madame Gilbert had opened the back door of the villa to let the cleaners in. Cami and her mother walked upstairs. Today they would tackle the third and fourth bedrooms and bathrooms.

Maybe the striking owner and his wife had other children who would be occupying these bedrooms, though he hadn't talked about any. The sight from the third bedroom window looked out on the property's greenery and outdoor pool. What a wonderful place to grow up.

When the owner had mentioned his son, she'd felt such love coming from him. A father's love was a great thing. She missed hers and turned away from the window to get busy.

After lunch in the van, her mother finished the third bathroom while Cami started on the fourth bedroom. As she was setting up, she heard a knock on the open door and turned her head to see the owner.

"I thought I'd better announce myself first before you saw me." That deep masculine voice of his curled its way through her insides. He brought in the ladder from the other room, which he set up for her.

"Thank you. My mother and I were going to bring it in."

"Now you don't have to. I'll move it wherever you wish. Just ask."

No man had ever looked so good wearing thigh-molding jeans and a T-shirt that covered his powerful shoulders and chest. This time it was her pulse that raced of its own volition.

She smiled. "I appreciate that. Since I wasn't up on it, I've been saved a trip to the hospital this afternoon." Before long she'd be going there for something that had nothing to do with a broken bone.

He laughed, exhibiting a refreshing sense of humor. "I should have asked your name yesterday."

"It's Camille Delon, but those who know me call me Cami."

He flashed her an answering smile. "*Bonne après-midi*, Cami. We weren't officially introduced yesterday. I'm Raoul Fontesquieu."

Raoul Fontesquieu? It couldn't be. But it had to be. There could only be one. She'd heard his name clearly over the radio.

Cami swallowed hard as reality set in. She clung to the side of the ladder where she stood. "I heard about the death of your grandfather. I'm so sorry. I never knew either of mine. You and your wife were lucky to have enjoyed him this long."

Her comment seemed to bring a subtle change in his demeanor, causing her to realize there were hidden emotions swirling inside of him. Prompted by his silence she said, "Let me congratulate you for being named the new CEO of your family's company. It was all over the news yesterday."

In an instant a frown broke out on his striking features. "I'm afraid bad news travels fast when it's false."

"What do you mean?" The comment had taken her back.

His lips twisted. "I'm divorced, and won't be accepting the position as CEO. In time, I won't be associated with the company at all. However, I'm assuming that the truth will be corrected before the week is out."

"Those are pretty colossal mistakes for the media to make." She was still trying to take it all in.

"Indeed." A strange smile appeared. "I came in here to ask if you would take a look at the nursery and tell me what you think about the color I've painted it. Is it too deep, or not light enough?"

It surprised her that he wanted her opinion at all. She couldn't help be excited. Everything about him had fascinated her even before she'd learned his identity. "Since I haven't started cleaning the ceiling yet, I'll come now."

Cami followed him down the hall. When they reached the entry, she took in the soft blue that had covered the off-white walls of the room. "It's perfect, monsieur. You did an excellent job. Are you sure you didn't head a house painting company in a former life?"

It was an outrageous comment to make knowing who he was, but she hadn't been able to resist. Not after realizing he was one of those royals her father had told her about years ago, even if their titles were defunct.

His laughter resonated in the room. Almost at once his body and expression relaxed, turning him back to the charismatic, virile man she'd hadn't been able to forget during the night.

"Call me Raoul, and tell me the truth."

"I promise you I just did," she assured

him with a smile. "The blue color you've chosen has created a soothing ambience any child would love. With the white cove moldings, I can picture the white furniture you picked out fitting in beautifully."

His black eyes gleamed. "Thank you. Now that I have your seal of approval, I'll have everything I've bought delivered on Friday. By Sunday I'll bring my son home to live with me permanently."

She could hear his excitement. "Where is he?"

He shifted his weight. "You've met Arlette Gilbert. She's his grandmother and has taken care of him from birth."

She blinked. But where was Madame Gilbert's daughter? According to the report on the radio, Raoul had been married to a woman named Sabine Murat. Cami was so confused.

By now she's learned enough to realize there were volumes of information he'd left out: like why his son hadn't lived with him from birth; why the divorce; where the birth mother was; what the reason was for the false news report that went out to the whole world.

But she didn't have the right to ask those questions. Cami was one of the cleaning ladies. In another couple of days, she'd never see him again.

"Your son is blessed to have a father like you who loves him so much and has painted his room. That's a story you can tell him when he's older. I lost my father at twelve."

"I'm sorry to hear that. You were so young."

"It was awful. For a while I thought my life was over. Hang on to the relationship with your son for dear life. Nothing's more important."

"I agree." Again, the emotion in his tone conveyed he was a man of deep feelings.

She turned to leave.

"Are you married, Cami?" With her gloves on, he wouldn't have noticed if she wore a ring or not.

She paused and looked back at him, surprised at the question. "I was married at eighteen and divorced at nineteen."

He studied her for a moment. "Do you have children?"

Cami shook her head. One month into

her marriage proved she'd made a mistake and she was glad she hadn't gotten pregnant. "I've been working ever since. Now I'd better get back to my cleaning."

His eyes played over her, sending darts of awareness through her. "Then I'll see you later."

For the rest of the afternoon she worked her head off. When she and her mother left the villa at five, the owner was nowhere in sight. On the way home she told her mom what she'd learned about him and the nursery he'd painted.

"So…he's a Fontesquieu… Like I said, money doesn't ensure happiness. A divorce? A little boy he's never lived with? Why on earth would he buy that large villa for the two of them when his home is the royal Fontesquieu Château? It doesn't make sense."

"Neither does the fact that he turned down the CEO position," Cami murmured. Most successful businessmen clamored their whole lives to achieve that status, but she already knew he wasn't like other men.

Raoul Fontesquieu was his own person. After telling her in a quietly fierce tone that the media had spread lies about him, he could no doubt be formidable on occasion.

Still, a tremor shook her body. Something had happened to her today, something she hadn't thought possible. His jaw-dropping appeal had taken her by surprise in a way that made her feel—oh, she didn't know—thrown off course when her path had been set for so long.

After they arrived at the apartment and ate dinner, Cami went to the store for a few groceries in their old black Citroën 2CV. It was on its last legs and looked like an umbrella, but it ran. She hoped it would help her find a way to clear visions in her head of the most devastatingly attractive man she'd ever met in her life!

Raoul met the pool contractor Wednesday morning. He walked him down the corridor from the kitchen. They passed the locked study and continued to the end of the house. The square-shaped tiled pool was sealed off with a sliding door.

The contractor brought in the supplies; a water kit, balancers, conditioners and chlorine tablets used to test the water. Raoul worked with him so he could do it himself from now on, then saw him out.

Before the applicants for the nanny job started to show up, Raoul took the staircase two steps at a time. He saw Cami in her safety glasses midway down the hall. Behind her he glimpsed one of the other workers cleaning a linen closet.

Cami was up on the ladder scrubbing the ceiling and moldings. Her loose-fitting hunter green T-shirt couldn't conceal the lovely shape of her body.

Afraid to startle her, he stayed where he was. When she saw him she waved with her free hand. "Bonjour, Raoul. It's okay to approach," she teased.

Amused, Raoul strode toward her. "I came to see how things are progressing. You've transformed the villa. It sparkles."

A smile broke out on her face, beguiling him. "That's good to hear. Our boss will be relieved."

He liked the way she fastened her black hair in a chignon that suited her oval face and high cheekbones. "Is she a slave driver?"

"Yes. Don't you agree, Maman?"

His gaze darted to the older brunette woman who'd just lifted her head and glanced at him from the closet. He saw the facial similarities and smiled at her. "You're all such hard workers, I'm impressed."

Both women chuckled. "Raoul? Meet my mother and best friend, Juliette Delon."

"Bonjour, madame."

"Bonjour, Monsieur Fontesquieu. It's nice to meet you. My daughter's right. Our boss cracks the whip, but she's nice."

"She's terrific," Cami chimed in.

Raoul admired their loyalty. "How refreshing to see a mother and daughter who work well together." He couldn't think of a single positive instance within the difficult female circles of the large Fontesquieu family. Years of living together under the roof of the château had done its damage. "I'm glad to have met you, Madame Delon. I promise to give all of you a top rating."

"We couldn't ask for more than that. It means work for another day," the pragmatic older woman commented before getting back to cleaning the shelves.

He couldn't imagine his ex-wife doing manual labor like this, let alone worrying about where her next euro was coming from. Naturally the comparison wasn't fair, but he couldn't help but be impressed by the Delons' work ethic.

"Don't let me keep you. I'll see you tomorrow." Already he knew he'd like to take Cami out to dinner so they could get better acquainted.

"Isn't your grandfather's funeral tomorrow?"

She'd remembered and had shown concern for his loss though he hadn't felt it himself. After living around his austere relatives, her natural warmth was like a healing balm. "Yes, but I'll be back in the afternoon."

Cami's thoughtful gaze met his briefly before he walked away. He'd have preferred to stay and talk, but not while she was working with her mother.

After going downstairs, he met with two applicants for the nanny position. Neither he nor Arlette were impressed.

Raoul had been guilt ridden over having to give up Antoinette, knowing the pain he'd caused her. He hadn't been there for the pregnancy he'd had no knowledge of.

Once he'd found out, he'd felt responsible for her death and the anguish he'd caused her and her family. On top of that he was well aware how deeply Arlette missed her daughter. Though she could have blamed Raoul, she'd never been anything but accepting and wonderful to him.

His latest worry was what kind of a father he was going to be. Could any nanny he chose measure up or tend Arlette's grandson with the love and care she and Minerve had provided?

This was a difficult decision for him to make, in truth the hardest of his life. He decided he'd made a mistake by not bringing Alain to the villa today. During the interviews, Raoul needed to watch the women interact with his son on a first meeting simply to see if there was any chemistry at all. If not, it might be a long time before he found the right person to take care of his precious boy.

Raoul could only hope one of the applicants sent to the villa tomorrow after three in the afternoon would stand out. He was also looking forward to spending more time with Cami. Besides her having an intrinsic charm that was growing on him, she had a way of encouraging him, of making him feel he could be a good father. Somehow he felt instinctively he could talk to her and connect.

CHAPTER THREE

THURSDAY HAD ARRIVED, which meant attending the funeral. Raoul climbed in the Mercedes. "Thanks for picking me up, Dom. Why isn't Nathalie with you?"

"We both felt the funeral was no place to introduce her to the family for the first time."

"I hear you."

"She wanted to go to Arlette's and help tend Alain. Arlette will be bringing him to your villa in time for the nanny interviews."

"What would I do without them?"

Dom flashed him a glance as they headed for the church. "They're so thrilled you two have been united, and that you're his father. They'd do anything for you. They love you."

"I don't deserve it."

"Never say that again. As far as I'm concerned, what Sabine did to you and Antoinette was evil."

Raoul agreed.

They pulled in the parking lot of the church where the hearse was parked. "I've been dreading today," Dom admitted.

Raoul groaned. "Tell me about it. Let's get this over."

The Fontesquieu family was laying a despotic patriarch to rest with all the grandeur of burying a king. Raoul couldn't take much more.

Both of them had dressed in black. They slipped in the back behind everyone else, refusing to join their individual families. Sabine, also in black with a veil, sat next to Raoul's parents with her family as if there'd been no divorce. They were all in denial. She turned her head when she saw them come in.

"Sabine never gives up, does she?" Dom said under his breath.

"Of course not," Raoul bit out. "I'm still waiting for Papa to inform the press of the truth. It's been five days…"

"He's waiting for you to come around."

Raoul shook his head.

Once the services were over, he and Dominic escaped out the back of the church with relief and walked to the Mercedes.

Between his cousin's private wedding where no Fontesquieu had been invited, plus the infuriating news that Raoul's divorce had gone through, not to mention his refusal to become CEO, they'd outraged both sets of parents and couldn't leave fast enough.

Everyone else would go on to the family cemetery on the eastern end of the estate to bury Armand Fontesquieu. All Raoul could think about was seeing Cami again. He couldn't wait to see her again and learn more about her. She was like a breath of fresh air.

Dominic dropped him off in front of the villa. Arlette had probably come and parked in back. The first thing Raoul did was hang his suit jacket and tie in the sitting room closet. After loosening the top buttons of his white shirt, he searched for Cami, nodding to some of the cleaners on the way.

Raoul found her in the large room he'd

designated for a playroom where Alain could bring his friends. It was down the same hall near the indoor pool. She'd put a drop cloth on the floor and was kneeling while cleaning the vents. He couldn't be more pleased to find her alone. Her mother had to be somewhere else cleaning.

"Mademoiselle Delon?" he said softly. Their eyes met. It made him glad to think she'd taken her maiden name, which meant she'd chosen not to keep her married name after her divorce. Obviously there'd been trouble in a marriage she'd chosen to forget. He and Cami already had something in common.

"I take it the funeral is over."

"*Oui*, thank heaven." He sat down by her and settled against the wall, resting his hands over his raised knees. "At least you weren't up on the ladder when I walked in."

She chuckled.

He undid the cuffs of his shirtsleeves and pushed them up to the elbows. "Can I help?"

"I'm almost through here." She lifted those heavenly eyes to him. "Are you all right?"

"I am now." Knowing she'd be here after the funeral had made his day. "I'm expecting a new applicant for the nanny job in a little while. Until then, give yourself a rest and put me to work."

"The way you're dressed, I wouldn't dream of it. This isn't a normal day for you. I'm aware you've just buried your grandfather and have turned down the CEO position. None of it could be easy for you."

He studied her for a moment, marveling at her capacity for understanding, even if she didn't know what was really going on inside of him. "This is probably going to shock you, but this has been a liberating day for me in so many ways you can't imagine. That may sound harsh to you, but I'm telling you the truth. Today I'm happier than I've been in years! My son's coming to live with me and a whole world has opened up. Since I feel like celebrating, I have an idea."

"What would that be?" Her engaging smile lit up his insides.

"If you're finished, why don't you come to the kitchen with me? We'll grab a drink and go into the sitting room to wait for the next woman to show up. You can help me vet her, maybe give me a signal one way or another what you think."

"As if I'd dare," she answered with a teasing tone.

"Why not? Once we're in there we'll have something comfortable to sit down on while we talk. All the furniture I've bought won't be delivered until tomorrow."

At his suggestion, she removed her gloves. "You once lived at the château, right?"

"All my life until now."

"What about the furniture you brought with you?"

"It went with my ex-wife." Including the two paintings Jerome had done years earlier and given to Raoul before his death.

She looked surprised, but didn't comment on it. "So in order to fill this villa, you've had to purchase *everything*?"

"That's right."

Her fabulous eyes widened. "You must have been shopping for ages."

"And having the time of my life. It's been a treat buying modern furniture that wasn't invented when the château was built. Alain wouldn't feel comfortable—"

"The way *you* weren't comfortable?" she surmised sotto voce. "I'm sorry. I shouldn't have said that."

"Don't be sorry. Your instincts are right." Cami was amazingly easy to talk to. They seemed so keyed into each other, it had caused him to let down his guard when he was with her.

"Still, please forgive me."

"There's nothing to forgive. You were only speaking the truth. The first time my cousin Dominic and I were throwing a ball around in his family's suite, we broke a statue by accident. Needless to say, that never happened again. Life at the château was never meant for children, let alone lively ones. The paintings and tapestries covered up what I always thought was a gigantic prison where children couldn't be themselves."

"And here I've found myself envying you."

"I've ruined your picture of life at the château, haven't I? But I'm afraid it was built and furnished for a very different period of time that was hard on children." Not waiting for a response from her, he got to his feet and put out his hands to help her stand.

"Thank you."

Together they walked through the house to the kitchen. He pulled two colas out of the fridge and left for the sitting room. She sat on the couch while he chose a chair.

"I haven't seen your mother, Cami."

"I think she and Marise are out cleaning the back patio. You didn't notice them?"

"My cousin drove us to the funeral and he dropped me off in front."

She nodded. "I hope this next interview for a nanny will produce the desired result."

He examined the features of her well-shaped nose. That enticing mouth was shaped like a budding rose. He longed to kiss her and it was starting to drive him mad. Again, he was shocked by his strong attraction to her. But it was too soon to be experiencing these feelings.

When he remembered how quickly his desire for Antoinette had taken over his life before fate stepped in to end their relationship, it worried him that history could repeat itself. Raoul needed to be careful not to rush into anything with Cami that could hurt her.

"That's my hope too. I'm excited about my new life." Right now, he was making a home for his son and establishing a new business. At least that was what he kept telling himself, but Cami was a raving beauty and her charisma had rubbed off on him. He found he couldn't be with her long enough to satisfy him.

"Everything you're doing has been based around your son in order to make him happy. He'll be a very lucky little boy," she asserted.

"Once I find the right nanny, one of my biggest worries will be solved. It's the worry about being a good father that gives me anxiety."

She flashed him one of those encouraging smiles. "The fact that it's your first thought guarantees you'll never fail. Papa always made me feel important."

The way Raoul's father and grandfather never did. Her hopeful, comforting words coincided with the ringing of the doorbell.

Disappointment swamped him for being interrupted. "That will be she. Just a minute."

He walked to the front door. "You're Monsieur Fontesquieu?" the brunette woman asked after he opened it. She kept staring at him.

"I am," he said. "Come in." He walked her into the sitting room. She was probably Cami's age. By now Cami had gotten to her feet.

Their eyes connected as they remembered what they'd said about vetting her. "Mademoiselle Delon? Let me introduce you to Mademoiselle Herve."

"How do you do, mademoiselle?"

The woman stared at Cami. "Does this mean *you're* the new nanny?" she blurted, surprising Raoul. "I thought the position hadn't been filled yet."

"It hasn't," Raoul declared, bringing the other woman's head around.

"If you'll excuse me, monsieur, I have a floor to clean. *À demain.*" Cami had been surprised too and couldn't escape fast enough. Raoul couldn't blame her.

He watched her leave the sitting room,

already regretting the fact that she'd gone back to her work.

Unfortunately he knew he hadn't found the right nanny for Alain yet. He hadn't yet put into words what he really wanted because he needed to be cautious when it came to getting involved with Cami. Again, after what had happened with Antoinette, he couldn't bear for Cami to be injured in any way because of him, but he could tell he was falling for her.

Cami's mother awakened on Friday morning, with a lot of pain in her right shoulder. "That does it, Maman. Yesterday you overdid it cleaning the patio and porch. Today you're staying home and taking care of yourself. There'll be four of us washing windows, so you don't need to worry. I'll see you tonight and bring dinner."

She kissed her mom and took off for her last day of work at the villa. After today she'd never see Raoul Fontesquieu again. It shouldn't matter to her, but she couldn't lie to herself. From the first day when he'd miraculously caught her in his arms, she hadn't been the same.

A man like him was unforgettable—and as out of reach as the stars in a distant galaxy whether she had a heart problem or not, which she did. He was the stuff that had made up her fantasies after visiting the Fontesquieu estate with her parents. She was supposed to have given those up.

You fool, Cami Delon.

When she reached the villa, she noticed a furniture truck out in front. Three men were unloading. Two of them carried a large box. She saw Madame Gilbert at the front door conducting traffic. Alain's grandmother held a trusted place in Raoul's heart. Naturally she did when he'd loved her daughter enough for a child to be born.

Experiencing a pang she shouldn't be feeling, Cami turned the van to head up the drive. As she passed, one of the men smiled at her with male interest, but no man could compare to the owner who'd already slipped past her defenses to make chaos of her emotions.

After parking around back, she entered the villa and found her coworkers in the kitchen. For their last job, they paired up. Cami and Patrice worked on the downstairs windows inside and out. By one o'clock, every pane in the villa had been cleaned and they were free to go. Madame Gilbert thanked them for their outstanding work before the four of them walked out in back to go home. Patrice and the others left first.

Cami got behind the wheel of her van. She'd brought a lunch, but since they'd finished work early, she would eat after she got home. After finding the keys, she started the engine. But Raoul suddenly appeared, blocking her way. Her heart jumped to her throat.

Shaking, she lowered the window. "I could have run you down!"

Laughter escaped. "I'm a little faster than that." His chiseled jaw and sensuous smile melted her bones. He came closer. With that black hair and those gleaming black eyes, he looked too marvelous in a navy pullover and khaki chinos.

"This is the first time I've seen you without your safety glasses. Has anyone ever told you those eyes are the exact lavender blue color of the flowers popping up in my family's vineyard?"

Heat surged to her cheeks. "Never, but

then I don't know anyone who's had an intimate knowledge of your vineyard."

"You know *me*."

Cami couldn't believe they were having this conversation.

"Before you go, I'd like you to see the nursery and tell me what you think. The furniture company delivered everything while you were cleaning windows this morning. Do you have time?"

How could she turn him down when he sounded this eager? Cami had to be honest with herself. She'd drawn closer to him so fast, she'd been disappointed to leave without at least seeing him once more to say goodbye.

"After telling me what you'd picked out, I'm curious to see the finished product."

He seemed happy with her answer and opened the door for her. They walked in the house. Several times their arms brushed, bringing a new awareness of him as they climbed the elegant staircase to the second floor.

"Oh—" she cried when they reached the nursery. She'd never seen a more delightful sight in her life!

The room contained the white furniture he'd talked about including a stand for diapers next to the dresser. There was also an adult rocking chair and a toy box. She spied a collection of toy cars and trucks in a basket with some other toys. Blocks filled another basket.

She loved the blend of the blue walls with white woodwork and white window shutters. A sand-and-ivory rug covered part of the pecan floor. All the wall prints and books in the bookcase added vibrant colors.

Cami chuckled over the French bulldog placed in a child's rocking chair. On a shelf in the bookcase she saw a blue-and-white toy sailboat.

She smiled at him. "This room is utterly enchanting, Raoul. What little boy in the world wouldn't want to claim it for his own?"

"I hope he'll learn to be happy here. I've spent part of every day with him since the grape harvest, but he's never lived with me."

Why? "To live morning, noon and night with his own papa who loves him? Surely you couldn't have any doubts." Yet Cami knew that he did and it tugged at her emotions to feel his vulnerability.

The sweetest sight of all was an exquisite quilt of nursery rhyme characters hanging over the end of the crib. She moved closer to examine it.

Raoul followed. "Alain's grandmother made several quilts before he was born. The other day she gave me this one for the nursery."

"It's absolutely beautiful!"

Cami looked up at him. *Where was the boy's mother?* She was dying to know.

"Antoinette died ten days after Alain was born." Raoul had read her mind after seeing the question in her eyes.

"Oh, no—" Cami put a hand to her heart. "How tragic." All this time she'd assumed Alain's mother was still alive somewhere.

"That's her picture on the dresser."

She glanced at the propped eight-by-ten framed photograph of a beautiful brunette woman.

His former lover.

"I want him to see her face every day."

"Of course." The man had to be in love

with her memory. His words brought a lump to Cami's throat.

"I didn't learn through Antoinette's stepsister Nathalie that I had an unknown son until this fall."

Unbelievable. Was the baby the reason for his divorce to the Murat woman? There was so much she didn't know about him. It was getting more complicated all the time. "How amazing and wonderful to be united with him."

His black eyes fused with hers. "You have no idea."

"Judging by this room you've created, I think I do."

"Thanks to you and your mother, plus the other women cleaning the villa, it's ready to be lived in. You'll all receive a bonus for your hard work and doing it so fast."

"It was fun." She flashed him another smile to hide what was going on inside of her. He still had to be suffering over the loss of the woman he'd loved. "We don't often clean a place as beautiful and exclusive as this. I'm sure you're going to be very happy here with your son." After a pause, "Did you hire Mademoiselle Herve? She seemed very eager for the job."

"You know very well I didn't. I'm afraid she was too eager and too impressionable."

"She was probably nervous about the interview." Though it was none of her business, Cami let out an inward sigh. The woman hadn't been able to take her eyes off Raoul. Not that Cami could blame her since she suffered from the same affliction. "Someone else will come along who's right for you and your son. Now I'm afraid I have to leave. My mother wasn't feeling well today."

"I'm sorry to hear that."

"It's her arthritis that acts up in her shoulders. I need to pick up some dinner for her and get home."

"Then don't let me keep you. I'll walk you out."

"You don't have to do that."

"What if I want to?"

His comment sent an unbidden dart of excitement through her. They went downstairs to the kitchen and out the back door. En route she discovered that while they'd been in the nursery, the kitchen furniture had been delivered. She'd spied a high chair, a table with six chairs and two stools placed at the island.

They continued walking outside. He opened the car door for her, then spoke to her through the open window. "What does a woman who cleans for NI do on a Saturday?"

"Clean the apartment."

He broke into rich male laughter. "The proverbial busman's holiday." She nodded, enjoying their conversation way too much. "Do you live alone?"

"With my mom."

His eyes studied her features for a moment. "Unless you have other plans tomorrow, would you help me clean my study? Naturally I'll pay you for your time. I'll do the ceiling if you'll do the walls."

She wondered why he hadn't left the room open while all of them had been cleaning during the week, but it wasn't any of her business. "I could come in the morning, but I have an appointment after lunch."

"Thank you. I appreciate it more than you know. We'll be done by noon. Now I'd better let you go. When you come tomorrow, park here and I'll leave the back door open." He backed away from the van so she could drive down to the street.

Each time she passed the entrance to the Fontesquieu estate, she thought about him. But this time it conjured up his comment about her eyes being the color of the flowers that grew there.

Cami didn't want to believe he was the kind of man who flirted with every woman he met, but maybe he was like that and had picked on her because it was so easy. Any woman young or old would be wildly attracted to him. Mademoiselle Herve had been a case in point. Cami wished *she* weren't. In fact she was upset that she'd agreed so easily to help clean his study in the morning.

There were some troubling facts about his past already staring her in the face. He'd had an affair with one woman that produced a child, yet he'd married another one. Now divorced, he was taking on the responsibility of fatherhood with the son of his lover.

Where did a cleaning lady fit in this scenario except to provide a momentary distraction for him? That was all she was or could be. Maybe he flirted in order to deal with his pain over losing Antoinette and could be forgiven. Who knew?

Cami had fallen out of love long before her divorce had been finalized. Any pain had more to do with her disgust for being such a bad judge of character. Since then she'd only gone on a few dates, but no man had interested her enough to get involved, not when she was facing heart surgery.

The only thing to do was be polite to the complicated man who'd given her and her mother a job for the week. Grateful for tomorrow's extra money, she'd do the cleaning and leave. Once out of sight, out of mind.

But to her chagrin Raoul wasn't out of sight during the night. He filled her dreams. She tossed and turned, and awakened on Saturday feeling restless and sick with excitement at the thought of seeing him again.

She climbed out of bed to get ready and fastened her hair back with a tortoiseshell clip. Once dressed in jeans and a blouse, she found her mother in the kitchen and told her she'd been hired to clean his study.

"That man is interested in you. What's nice is, you're interested in him too. Have a good time."

Cami ignored her mother's comments. "I'll be back by one to get you." The two of them were going to do some shopping for friends and extended family. This was one of the few free times left before her operation. "It will be my *last* trip to the villa."

"Are you sure of that, because I'm not," she quipped.

Cami left the apartment afraid her mother was right. If he happened to ask her for another favor, she probably wouldn't be able to resist.

Saturday morning Raoul opened the back door when Cami's car appeared. Every time he saw her, it was like the first time. She had an inner and outward beauty that appealed to him on every level.

"Bonjour, Cami. Thanks for coming to help me." He walked her inside and headed for the study. He'd lined up the furniture and boxes along the hallway.

They made their way past everything to enter the room where he'd placed a drop cloth and ladder. There was a door at the end of the room that led outside to the driveway.

"I was up early and finished most of the ceiling. You're free to start the walls. I don't think this will take us long."

Her lavender-blue eyes were charged with excitement. She put on the safety glasses and gloves to get busy. "You've done the hardest part."

"This is nothing compared to what you and your coworkers accomplished this last week. When I bought this place, I knew it needed a thorough going-over and felt sorry for you."

"It wasn't bad, Raoul. The people who lived here before left it reasonably clean. Try cleaning a half-burned house. That's a real nightmare."

Her life hadn't been easy. "I can only imagine." Once done, he climbed down and put the ladder out in the hall.

As soon as she finished the last wall, he rolled up the drop cloth and cleaned the floor. "We make a good team," he announced at last. They stood in the doorway. "The room is ready to furnish."

She eyed the oak desk. "You're going to need help moving this."

"I'll do it. Leave the heavy lifting to me."

Cami had no choice because of her heart condition, but it didn't matter. His tall, hard, fit body could handle anything and was probably the envy of most men. No woman could keep her eyes off him.

While he brought in the furniture and told her to sit on the love seat, she was able to watch him. He also brought in a file cabinet and more chairs before he pulled a framed picture out of the desk and set it on top. At the first sight of the two people in the photo, she let out a cry.

He turned to her. "What's wrong?"

"I don't believe it," she whispered and got up to get a closer look. "That's *you* with that older man!"

Raoul chuckled. "Yes, but what do you mean?"

She stared up at him, incredulous. "*You're* the young man I saw at the vineyard with this older man years ago!"

"You saw *me*? With *this* man?" He tapped the picture.

"Yes. I was twelve. I was in the car with my mother and father. We'd stopped to watch the grape pickers. You and he were walking through the vineyard talking to the workers before you headed toward a big black car waiting at the side of the road. It had a gold hood ornament."

"That was a special day for me."

"For me too. I asked my papa about the emblem and he said it meant you belonged to the Fontesquieu family. You happened to smile at me before you got in. Good heavens! *That's* why your smile seemed familiar to me on Monday when we first met in the nursery."

Raoul stared hard at her. "*You* were the pretty girl with the long glossy hair watching me from the back window. You reminded me of a black-haired Rapunzel. I couldn't figure out what you were doing inside a taxi."

She laughed. "My twelve-year-old self decided then and there you were the young prince who lived in the château."

"That's incredible." He rubbed the back of his neck. "Even though you're grown up and your hair has been caught back, it must explain why I felt drawn to you in those first moments. We had a connection."

"I agree," she murmured. "Who's the man in the picture with you?"

"My great uncle Jerome, the man I've talked about. It was my birthday. I'd just turned fifteen and his wife took that picture of us when we returned to the château from inspecting that particular terroir in the vineyard. They'd planned a surprise for me that evening. It was one of the happiest nights of my life."

She nodded. "Seeing that photograph takes me back to a time of great happiness with my parents too. From the time I was five, Papa always took us to the vineyard in the fall. It was one of my favorite things to do with him, but because certain roads were blocked off, we could never get close enough to the château to suit me. Then he'd drive us around Vence and relate stories about its history."

"Give me a for instance," Raoul urged her. "I love hearing about your childhood."

"I remember him saying that Francis the First, the knightly prince who furnished the ash tree that still grows near the fountain in the city, loved his mother so much, he knelt before her whenever they talked."

Raoul cleared his throat. "I didn't know that fact about his mother."

"Do you think it's true?"

"We'll never know, but it makes a tender story."

"Yes. Papa loved history and knew a lot of things. He should have lived for a long time." Her voice wobbled before she sat back down.

"His legacy lives in you, Cami. Your words have touched me to the core." He walked out in the hall and started bringing in the large boxes containing a computer and printer. Then he brought in the smaller boxes.

"Shall I help unpack those? I'm still on your clock for another hour. Let me be useful."

"Your work ethic is as unmatched as your energy. Make yourself comfortable and we'll go through them. Before we do though, I'll bring us some coffee and then we'll get started."

"That would taste good about now."

CHAPTER FOUR

ENCOURAGED THAT CAMI didn't want to leave, Raoul hurried to the kitchen and made a fresh brew. His mind kept going over the things she'd told him. The mention of the knight's mother made him realize he needed to call his own mother and try to make things better between them.

He hadn't sat next to her at the funeral, but that was because Sabine had been right there. Even if his mother understood, he wanted to explain and Cami's words reminded him he shouldn't put it off.

Filling a plate with pastries, he carried everything to the study and handed her a mug. The pastries he put on the desk, then he pulled up a chair.

She reached for one and bit into it. "Um. Just what the doctor ordered."

Raoul swallowed his coffee, then studied

her for a moment. "I can tell you're wondering why I kept this room locked while you and your coworkers were cleaning."

A fetching half smile appeared. "Am I that transparent?"

"You know that old saying about eyes being mirrors of the soul."

"Afraid I do. I'll keep them closed from here on out."

Low laughter rumbled out of him. Raoul knew he was in terrible trouble where she was concerned. It was too soon to be this enamored, but he couldn't help it and decided it was time to do something about it.

"If you remember, I told you I wouldn't be accepting the CEO position."

She drank her coffee slowly. "I remember everything you told me."

"That's because I've gone into business for myself, but it's still a secret. I put these boxes in here last week and locked the door. I didn't want anyone coming to the villa and getting curious." He opened the first one and pulled out some files.

"Why are you telling *me*?"

He gave her a long side glance. "After what we've just shared, I trust you."

"That's a real compliment. Are they in alphabetical order?"

"No."

"Would you like me to arrange them?"

"Please."

She took them one at a time and made a pile next to her. "That was easy. Why don't you open another box?"

Once they got started, there was no stopping her. Soon all the boxes had been emptied and she'd put all the files in the cabinet.

"You did that fast," he commented.

She flicked her gaze to him. "Are these boxes from your office?"

"This *is* my office."

"You know what I mean."

His lips twisted into a smile. "I'm head of Fontesquieu Marketing and Sales for only a few more days. Then my ties will be severed from the whole family business."

She bit her lip. "Doesn't that disturb you a little?"

Her insights were a revelation. "If you want to know the truth, I can't wait. I've started a new company and have sent ads throughout Provence. From here on I'll be doing all business here at the villa."

"So *that's* why you didn't accept the CEO position."

One dark brow lifted. "No. That's not the reason. I would never want to be the head of the family business under any circumstances. At this point I intend to be my own man. One of the reasons I chose to buy this villa was because this study has an outdoor exit and parking around the back for clients."

"I noticed."

"It makes everything convenient without involving the rest of the household."

"Of course." She cocked her head. "Do you mind if I ask what your new business is about?"

"For years I've wanted to build a consultancy firm for people who desire to start their own vineyard, but don't know where to begin."

Cami blinked. "Kind of like their own private expert."

He smiled. "That's one way of putting it."

"You'd rather do something like that than continue to work for your family?"

"In truth, I've wanted to do it for years."

"Your knowledge will be invaluable!" she cried.

Her excitement sent chills over his body. "Maybe."

"There's no maybe about it."

He stared at her. "Why do you say that?"

"Every time I've ever driven past your family's vineyard, I've wondered how it got started and how your family continued to make it flourish over the centuries.

"To me it seems like an impossible project that would take someone brilliant to start a whole new vineyard and make it work. But you know all its secrets! No one would ever go wrong consulting you. There'd be no risk."

"There are risks, Cami, and it takes a lot of work."

"But they'd be learning from your genius."

"My great uncle was the genius. I need the journals he kept to help me, but they're with my ex-wife. One day I'll get them." A dark brow lifted. "Anytime you want, you're welcome to head my advertising department."

A gentle laugh escaped before she glanced

at the cabinet. "So those files represent the people who've already responded to your ads."

"That's right."

"You've received a lot already."

"We'll see how much it grows. I've advertised under an old family name Degardelle that has no connection with the Fontesquieu family. I won't be giving away any family secrets, but I know enough about the art of raising grapevines to help others. I want something that my son can get involved in one day, if it's what he wants."

Her eyes lit up, intensifying their unique color. "He'll want to do everything *you* do, I promise you. As you now know, my papa was a *chauffeur de taxi.* As a little girl, I had a dream of owning my own taxi."

"After what you've told me, that doesn't surprise me."

"I imagined driving all sorts of interesting, fascinating people around. That was until Papa drove us to your family's estate and I saw the château for the first time from a distance."

One black brow quirked. "What happened then?"

"I thought we'd come to the land of enchantment. As I told you a few minutes ago, I imagined being the princess who lived inside with her prince."

Cami had no comprehension what this conversation was doing to him. In an earlier time, he would have loved living in the château with her. "How long did that dream last?"

"After Papa died, it stopped, but he always had the most influence over me. I'm sure your son will want to follow in your footsteps. That's how it works. Now I have to go." She stood up.

Enthralled by her conversation, the last thing he wanted was for her to leave. She had yet to tell him about the rest of her life, her failed marriage, but now wasn't the moment to detain her. She had an appointment.

"I'll walk you out."

"Please don't bother. You've got all your computer equipment to put together. You have no idea what a pleasure it's been to work here for you. I'm glad we met and I wish you all the happiness in the world with your son."

That was a goodbye speech if Raoul had ever heard one, but he had news for her and followed her through the villa to her car. "This may be your last workday with me, but I want to go on seeing you. Tomorrow I have to run by my old office on the estate and would like to take you with me. You'll be able to see the château up close."

He'd caught her off guard. "You mean it?"

"Knowing how much you loved your father, I'm certain another visit there will have special meaning for you. I'll be with my son part of the day, so I was thinking five o'clock. I'd really like to do this for you. All I need is your address."

He could hear her mind working, but was having a heart attack waiting for her answer. Finally, "How can I possibly say no to an invitation that would mean the world to me? I'll be outside at five. I live in an eight-plex at 130 Almond Street."

Relief swept through him. "I'll be there." As he helped her get in, he brushed her lips briefly with his own before shutting the door.

* * *

Raoul's quick kiss had come as a breath-taking surprise. The touch of his mouth on hers had kept her restless all night. She was still shaken when she got up on Sunday.

Cami could no longer pretend her deepest feelings weren't involved. Meeting this man who was bigger than anything life had really thrown her. He'd created feelings in her she didn't want to have, let alone feelings she didn't believe were hers to have!

Her mom had gone out with friends earlier. Cami left a note that Raoul was going to show her the château up close this evening, but she wouldn't be late. He had his little boy to get home to. Her mother's prophecy had come true. Cami couldn't stay away.

After washing her hair, she used the blow-dryer and left it loose and curly around her shoulders. While she put on her makeup, she realized she was a far cry from Rapunzel, the golden-haired princess high up in the tower.

She put on a wraparound blue skirt and matching sweater. After grabbing her jacket, she left the apartment a few minutes early and went outside to wait. When she saw the gleaming red Jaguar pull up in front, she sucked in her breath.

Raoul got out and helped her in the passenger side. He wore a burgundy-colored pullover sweater and dark gray trousers. One covert look at him and he'd become the embodiment of her fictional, dark-haired prince living at the château.

His black eyes played over her. "You should wear your hair long more often. It's stunning," he said before driving them down the street toward the main route leading up into the hills. His compliment had her trembling.

Cami whispered her thanks, but found it hard to comprehend that when she'd thought she'd never see him again, he'd invited her to come with him this evening. If they were headed for a relationship, her feelings for him were already over the top.

"How is your son? Did you bring him home?"

"I did, and we've been having the time of our lives. Nathalie is with him now."

"I'm thrilled for you."

Within a few minutes their drive brought them to the gate of the famous Fontesquieu estate. He turned in. Suddenly it was déjà vu. In the distance the fantastic château came into view.

"I can't believe this has been your home all your life."

"It was like living in a large zoo under one roof. In comparison, my villa is paradise."

He'd packed so much emotion into those statements, Cami felt saddened and stirred in her seat. "Every time my father brought me and my mom here, I wondered about the people who lived inside."

Raoul darted her a glance. "Besides your prince?"

Cami laughed quietly. "I was a child with a big imagination and can be forgiven."

"I assure you no prince or princess lived here. We were the same, difficult, ordinary people who live in apartments and houses throughout the world with the same flaws and imperfections that make up part of the human family."

"Please don't destroy all my illusions. I'd like to keep a few."

He chuckled. "The public isn't allowed inside, but I'll drive us around on those forbidden roads so you can see it up close."

"Where were you when we needed you?" she teased.

He reached over and squeezed her hand. It shot warmth through her body before he slowly let it go, leaving her bereft. Soon they'd come to the private road that circled next to the base of the magnificent structure.

"Does your whole family still live here?"

"You mean my grandmother, my parents, six aunts and six uncles, eighteen cousins, twelve nieces, ten nephews and a load of great grandchildren?" He pulled the car to a stop and flashed her that heart-stopping smile. "Then yes. In fact every one of them except for my cousin Dominic and myself."

She couldn't imagine it. "Does that mean you two are the rebels?"

"The family considers us the black sheep. Is it any wonder I've found pure peace at the villa?"

More than ever Cami realized what an enormous change he'd gone through to separate himself from the world he'd been born into. Her eyes took in the architecture that made the château so spectacular. "Where was your room when you were young?"

"On the third floor in the center right up there." He pointed.

She didn't want to ask where he'd lived with Sabine. "There have to be so many fun places to explore."

"Fun, yes, but I paid a price when I got caught."

Cami frowned. "Why?"

"My grandfather ruled supreme and everyone obeyed him. He wouldn't tolerate a child being a child, especially me or Dominic whom he called the ringleader since he was a year older. No noise. No friends allowed inside the château. Any play had to be done outside under supervision, and those friends had to be handpicked by our fathers because they considered us serious problems who needed discipline."

"No wonder you're so fond of Dominic."

"He and I grew closer than brothers to survive our childhood. If we did something wrong, we were separated for a week from playing together. We were also locked in our rooms without food for twelve hours so we would come to our senses."

Cami was scandalized. "Are you kidding me?"

He lifted his hands. "I swear."

"My father was so sweet to me, I feel terrible for what you had to suffer."

"That was a long time ago. If you've seen enough, I'll drive over to the office. It'll only take me a minute."

To her surprise it was housed in a large modern building behind the château. Being a Sunday, the parking lot had few cars. She marveled over the incongruity of new and old in the same panorama sweep.

He parked in front and got out. "I'll be right back."

She watched him stride inside on those strong powerful legs. No man could ever measure up to him, inside or out. He had hold of her heart.

Sure enough he returned quickly. After he climbed in behind the wheel, his smile made her feel all fluttery inside.

"Did you get what you came for?"

"I needed this." He showed her a thumb

drive before putting it in his shirt pocket. "This contains valuable new client information I couldn't find earlier and didn't want anyone else getting hold of. On our way out of here I'll drive you through one of the vineyards where tourists come to taste our wine. We'll stop there for a bite to eat too. How does that sound?"

"You know how much I'd love it." Cami would have gone anywhere with him for as long as he wanted. Her moment of truth had come. She was absolutely crazy about him. It was hard to believe a man like him existed.

The rows of vines were perfectly aligned and didn't look real. It thrilled her to think he was going to help would-be vintners to choose the right property and soil in order to grow grapes. His expertise would guarantee he'd make a huge success of his new company. Cami had no doubt he'd be touted forever. It was a privilege to know him.

Her eyes widened when he slowed down near a château much smaller than the main one that offered the delights of the Fontesquieu vineyard to the public. There were dozens of cars surrounding the structure.

"One of my jobs growing up was to run this place one summer."

"Did you like it?"

"Let's just say I learned a lot toward my later job of becoming head of Sales and Marketing. It surprised me how many people, women and men, love to talk about wine, the dreams they have about the perfect wine and what they prefer. Some of them wanted to start a vineyard of their own. I gained insights I wouldn't have had otherwise. But enough about the past. It's time to feed you and enjoy a little wine."

Little did Raoul know it, but he'd fed her in so many ways today, she never wanted any of it to end.

He led her around the side to a private entrance that took them inside a tasting room with arched ceilings and all sorts of signs with writings about wine. She found it fascinating.

Raoul found them a table, and an aproned man at the bar walked over. "*Eh bien*, Raoul. What can I get for you?" The man's gaze kept eyeing Cami.

"Your tapas and drinks from my special *bouteille*."

"Tout de suite."

"Auguste couldn't keep his eyes off you," Raoul whispered after the other man had gone.

"You're imagining things." But his comment excited her. She started looking around and began laughing when she read one of the signs near their table.

Raoul smiled. "Which one amuses you?"

"The Baudelaire quotation."

Without looking at it he said, "One should always be drunk. That's all that matters. But with what? With wine, with poetry, or with virtue as you choose. But get drunk!"

They both laughed. When it stopped, the way he was looking at her made her senses swim. For the next half hour they ate delicious fish hors d'oeuvres and sipped his favorite rose sherry.

"Try it," he urged her, studying her mouth.

"All right." She drank a little. "Um. It's really delicious."

"Can you detect the rich, ripe fruit flavors of vanilla, strawberry, pomelo and tangerines?"

"I think I can taste strawberry."

He smiled. "I find this particular vintage at it's perfect sweetness." He leaned closer to brush his lips against hers. "Almost as sweet as your mouth glistening from the sherry."

His kiss turned her body to liquid and she was so entranced, she forgot the time. But it had to come to an end.

Raoul took her to the car and they left for her apartment. Filled with good food and wine, she couldn't bear to have to say good-night, but his son would be waiting for him at the villa. Cami knew Raoul was anxious to get home to him.

He cupped her elbow as he walked her to the apartment door. She raised her eyes to him. "Thank you for the private tour of your estate and the delicious dinner. I'll remember it always."

"I'll never forget this Sunday evening either. Expect a call from me tomorrow. We have a lot to talk about." In the next breath he lowered his head and gave her a lingering kiss she couldn't help but respond to before he strode swiftly to his car.

Cami stood there shaking from the sensations he'd aroused in her before she found the strength to go inside. Her mom still wasn't back yet, but it was only ten, which was just as well. Cami wanted to go to bed and savor what had happened this evening.

Raoul returned to the villa, aching with desire for Cami. He had plans for them tomorrow, but when he sat down at his computer before going to bed, he faced a mass of emails from clients he'd serviced over the years. They were waiting for him to get back from vacation so life could return to normal with him overseeing everything.

Raoul should have anticipated that reaction and realized it was time to clarify his situation. First, he called the Fleur-de-Lis Hotel in Fréjus. After reserving their largest conference room for tomorrow afternoon and evening, he reserved two rooms for Monday night.

With that done he phoned Jean-Pierre to tell him what was going on. It was time to make his cousin's position official as head of Sales and Marketing.

Between the two of them they sent emails throughout Provence to as many clients who could come. Those who couldn't make it would hear about it. Though it was short notice, he decided it was better to put out the fire ASAP. The move would be a fait accompli by the time his father heard about it.

On Monday morning he got up early to feed Alain and swim with him. Nathalie had stayed the night and agreed to stay for the day After the three of them had lunch, he packed and left for the thirty-minute drive to Fréjus.

En route he sent Cami a text that he'd gone out of town, but would call her on Tuesday to make plans. She'd be cleaning so he didn't want to bother her with a phone call. It was hard to have to wait another day to see her, but he needed to get this out of the way.

Jean-Pierre met him and they set up the large room. Before long the clients trickled in. The place was soon filled, which was very satisfying to Raoul. These were men and women he'd worked with for years.

When it was time, he walked up to the microphone. "Thank you for coming on such short notice, but my life has completely changed and you deserve to know what's going on.

"I have a son named Alain who's almost nineteen months old. He's come to live with me for good while I've been on vacation. I've entered a new phase of my life as a single man and can no longer work for the family business. He needs my full attention. But I know you're going to approve of my successor. After dinner is served, we'll both be on hand to talk to all of you."

He turned to his cousin. "Jean-Pierre Fontesquieu? Come on up here so I can officially introduce you as head of Marketing and Sales for the entire Fontesquieu Company. Not only are we cousins, we've worked together for years. He's been in charge while I've been on vacation and is the man who has my backing 100 percent."

As everyone stood and clapped, Raoul patted him on the shoulder. "It's your turn," he whispered with a smile.

No one could know what it meant to have this over and done. He truly was free now to embrace his new life with his son and the woman who was already necessary to his existence.

CHAPTER FIVE

ON MONDAY AFTERNOON Cami received the disappointing text that Raoul was out of town and would call her tomorrow. That must have been a sudden move on his part. She hoped he was all right. Somehow she got through the rest of the day, but couldn't wait until she saw him again.

Her sense of loss had grown acute by the time she and her mom returned to the apartment at the end of the day. No sooner had they walked inside than their neighbor Suzanne, the widow next door, was at the door.

"These flowers arrived for you. Just a minute. There are more." She was back in a minute. "Lucky you! Now I have to run, but I want to hear the story behind these later."

They thanked her and put the flowers on

the coffee table. Cami took the paper off the first one. A gasp escaped her lips when she saw a vase filled with a dozen long-stemmed lavender roses, so exquisite they took her breath.

Another cry came from her mother who'd discovered a basket of yellow daisies called marguerites that looked like summer. She looked up at Cami.

"Is there any doubt where these came from?"

Cami smelled the roses with their heavenly bouquet. At this rate, that bad heart of hers needed an operation tomorrow. "No."

"That must have been quite an evening you had at the vineyard with Raoul Fontesquieu last night."

"He took me to see the château up close and then we had a meal at the wine-tasting château."

Her mother smiled. "And on Saturday you helped him clean his study."

Cami nodded.

"He not only looks the part, he's every woman's idea of perfection."

Don't remind me, Maman.

She reached for the card inserted in the roses.

"What does it say?" her mom asked.

"*'You've brought light into my life. R.'*"

A little shiver ran through her body before Cami glanced at her mother. "What did he write to you?"

"*'Thank you for an outstanding job despite the pain in your shoulders. Raoul Fontesquieu.'*" She eyed Cami with uncommon interest. "He says and does everything right, doesn't he?"

"Yes. But what you've just said makes me suspicious. It's all happening too fast."

"Why do you look so troubled?" her mother prodded. "Does this have anything to do with your ex?"

"Maybe somewhere deep down I don't trust my own feelings after my bad marriage."

"Then talk to me. Come on."

Cami sank down on one of the chairs, remembering the last kiss Raoul had given her. She still trembled from it. "He walked me to the door and said he'd call me today. Then he sent a text that he'd gone out of town.

"Now I see these roses. I feel like I'm

spinning out of control and still have so many questions about him."

Her mother sat down opposite her. "Like what?"

"For starters, he has a toddler son he only learned about this fall. In the nursery he's put a picture on the dresser of his lover who died after the baby was born. He's barely divorced. I have no idea if he was unfaithful to his former wife or not.

"I can't help but wonder how many other vulnerable women have been left in his wake—women hoping for life everlasting with a man like him. The nanny who came for an interview couldn't take her eyes off him. Her behavior reminded me of myself."

"Give it time and you'll learn a lot more about him."

"I'm afraid to learn more and then find out I was a detour along the way." Cami was already disturbed at the thought of his losing interest in her. "It might be better if I never see him again, that is if he calls me again." He would haunt her dreams forever, but she didn't dare open herself up for possible heartache when she was already facing a personal health crisis.

Her mom walked over and hugged her. "Christophe hurt you."

"At first, Maman. But after I realized I'd made a terrible mistake to marry him, I was no longer in pain. He was a child and always will be. With hindsight I realized I'd gone into that marriage so young because I'd wanted security after losing Papa. Christophe was too immature to handle any crisis, especially the fact that my heart murmur wasn't getting better."

A wince marred her mother's brow.

"On the surface, Raoul Fontesquieu appears to be heaven's gift to women and has more money than most of us can imagine. But because of my former experience, I need to be aware of the warning signs—like that picture of his lover—and not get any more involved with him.

"Soon my life will be going in a brand-new direction. Depending on a positive result of my operation, which I worry about, I'll be working at Gaillard's, and be able to take care of both of us. You need a rest."

"That's not your job, Cami."

"Why not? You've sacrificed for me all these years. It's my turn."

"But there will come a time when—"

"I don't think so, Maman," she interrupted her. "I have to get through the operation first and find out the chances for survival. Forget thinking about a mythical man in my future. He would have to be the antithesis of someone like Raoul Fontesquieu with his complicated life and background.

"His type comes from another planet, let alone a different cultural postal code from mine, and has so much family baggage you can't wade your way through it. I have to face reality. If a man does show up—that is if I have a future—and he isn't trustworthy or can't add richness to the solid life I'm planning to establish, then I don't want him under any circumstances."

She kissed her mom. "I'm going to get ready for bed and read for a while. We're facing another workday tomorrow. Get a good sleep."

"Don't you want to put the flowers in your bedroom?"

"It wouldn't be a good idea."

Cami went back to her bedroom deep in thought. At eighteen she'd thought marriage would make her blissfully happy. How wrong could she have been? Shouldn't she have learned some lessons that would prevent her making another serious mistake?

On Saturday while she'd been arranging those files in his study, for a moment she'd found herself fantasizing about the tall, dark, prince-like Raoul Fontesquieu on the opposite end of the spectrum. There was no question he seemed to be and have everything she'd dreamed about after her father had taken them to see the château and grounds. But there was a glaring divide that excluded her.

He was born to that billionaire class of people and culture who could have whatever they wanted, who'd recently divorced with a love child in tow from the beautiful woman whose picture sat on Alain's dresser.

Raoul was obviously estranged from his family and the stories he'd told her explained why. Any day now he expected to cut himself off from them. There had to be serious trouble inside that dynasty for the media to print news about him that wasn't true. Since their conversation, she understood why he didn't want to live in the château that was a treasure of France, an iconic symbol some people would sell their souls to inhabit.

Even with her empathy for him, could she bring herself to trust a man like Raoul Fontesquieu? How would he react if he knew about her heart condition? Right now he was attracted to her. Would his attraction for Cami be fleeting until he found another woman he wanted to be with? Possibly one from his own strata?

Cami had made up her mind that until her heart gave out, she needed to survive in her own strata. If she couldn't become independent on her own, then she would have no one to blame but herself. With her father gone and a marriage dissolved a long time ago, she'd be a fool to go on trusting her growing feelings for Raoul if he didn't feel the same way. Part of her felt like she didn't have the right to his love.

On Tuesday Cami left for work with her mom. Raoul said he'd call her today. Maybe, maybe not. She missed him horribly and began to wonder if those roses had been his way of saying goodbye to her, just as she'd feared.

While she and her mom sat out in the van to eat lunch, her phone rang. It made her jump before she pulled it out of her purse and discovered it was Raoul. Just the sight of his name started her heart thumping.

"If that's who I think it is, I'll go inside while you answer it." Her mother was out of the car in an instant.

Cami clicked On. "Raoul?" She tried to keep the tremor out of her voice.

"I hope it's the right time to phone you."

"Of course. I'm eating my lunch."

"I would have called sooner but I've been out of town and just got back. The villa isn't the same without you being here. Are you free tonight? I thought we'd take a drive along the *côte* and eat dinner somewhere. There are things I want to talk about with you."

Her body reacted as if she'd suddenly been hit by a bolt of electricity. "I'd love to do that." Despite all her fears, she realized there weren't many more days before her operation. She had to admit she wanted to spend every free moment with Raoul.

"How soon can you be ready?"

"By six thirty."

"Perfect. *À tout à l'heure, ma belle.*"

He'd never used an endearment like that with her before. She hung up so excited, her feet hardly touched the ground as she went back in the house to join her mother. On their way home at the end of the day, Cami told her that Raoul was taking her out for the evening. She could tell her mother was happy about it.

Before he picked her up, she showered and washed her hair, leaving it loose. After blow-drying it, she picked out a skirt and sweater in shades of tan and white and spent time doing her makeup.

This time Cami waited until he came to the door. She invited him in because her mother wanted to thank him for the flowers. Once he'd ensconced her in the car, she turned to him.

"As my mother told you, she loved her marguerites. No one has sent her flowers since Papa died. You couldn't have done anything nicer for her."

"That's because I'm grateful for all your hard work."

"Those lavender roses are so exquisite, they take my breath away."

"I have the same reaction when I look into your eyes. I'm glad you like them. If the hyacinths in the vineyard were in bloom, I'd have sent you an armful."

"You're much too generous."

He started the car and they headed for the main route out of Vence. "You have no idea how I've been living for this evening. I thought we'd drive to Beaulieu and eat dinner on the water at a wonderful little spot that serves delectable cod croquettes you'll love."

"I was already hungry before you told me that."

"Good. The whole time I was in Fréjus, I was planning out what we'd do when I got back."

"What were you doing there?"

"News of my leaving the family business has reached all our clients. Some have been upset, so I arranged for a conference to meet with many of them and introduce them to Jean-Pierre."

"How did it go?"

"Very well."

She eyed him steadily. "No one could ever measure up to you, Raoul. I'm not surprised they're upset."

"No one boosts my confidence the way you do." He reached for her hand and held it all the way to the sea. His warmth spread through her body.

The delightful little restaurant in the coastal village looked magical with its patio heaters. The place was crowded, but Raoul had reserved them a table overlooking the water. True to his word, the cod was out of this world, as was the Fontesquieu wine he'd handpicked.

"I have a confession to make," he said after they'd finished their meal.

Cami had no idea what was coming next.

"I almost phoned your manager at NI on Saturday to ask her to talk to you on Monday about being my part-time housekeeper until you left for the holidays on the sixteenth."

Cami was stunned by the news.

"I planned to tell her I needed one and wondered if you'd like the position. It's true that I need someone on the premises now that I'm working at home. Not all day every day. Maybe twice a week. Arlette served that purpose for the last two weeks, but she's back working at her pharmacy now."

Somehow that was the last thing Cami would ever have expected to hear. She averted her eyes. For a moment she was speechless. *And hurt.* She'd thought—oh, she didn't know exactly what she'd thought, but it wasn't to take over for Arlette!

She'd thought it odd when he'd asked her to help clean his study on Saturday. What did he *really* want? Cami had done nothing but think about him since Sunday night. Now this—What was going on?

"Raoul—"

"Don't say anything," he interrupted her. "I only told you this to let you see how desperate I am to be with you morning, noon and night. Surely by now you must realize you're the woman I'm so attracted to. I only want to be with you.

"For the week you were cleaning, I knew I'd see you every day. But after it was over, I didn't want it to end so I thought up the idea of asking you to be my housekeeper.

But of course, that's not what I want at all. Now you know the truth of my feelings."

In the last minute he'd taken her emotions on a giant roller coaster ride. While she was still trying to catch up to the fact that he wanted a relationship with her, he said, "I hope it's clear that I need to be with you as much as possible, but I know you have to work during the day. The only solution is to be with you every evening and on weekends or I'm not going to make it. Please tell me you want the same thing."

She took a deep breath. "I wouldn't be having dinner with you tonight if I'd wanted to stop seeing you."

"*Dieu merci* for that. Come on. I'll drive you home because I know work comes early for you in the morning."

They walked back out to his car. She felt like she was in a dream. He reached for her hand once more and clung to it all the way to the apartment. At the front door he drew her into his arms and kissed her thoroughly. Cami couldn't get enough of him.

"Thank you for this evening, Raoul. I do love being with you."

He buried his face in her hair. "Tomorrow will you come to the villa after your work and bring your bathing suit?"

"Is your indoor pool ready to use?"

"Yes. You can help me christen it with Alain."

She finally eased away from him, but it was almost impossible to stop kissing him back. "That's exciting. I'll probably get there by five thirty."

"I'll leave the back door unlocked for you. I can't wait," he murmured before walking out to his car.

Cami went inside and closed the door.

"Cami?"

She reeled around. "I'm home."

Her mother walked into the salon in her robe and sat in a chair. "How was your evening?"

Cami couldn't lie to her mom and sank down on the couch. "Wonderful." She told her what he'd said about wanting to hire her for his housekeeper before admitting to the real reason why. "Sounds like Raoul is infatuated, and has been totally honest with you. Have you told him about your heart condition?"

"No."

"That's because of your ex's reaction."

The problem with talking to her mother was that she knew Cami's fears and secrets way too well and was about as subtle as a sledgehammer.

"Christophe knew I had a heart murmur, but he never thought about it until after we were married and he wanted me to do one of those fun run marathons with him. When I told him I couldn't, he freaked out when he heard the reason why and wouldn't even talk to me about it sensibly. He didn't treat me the same after that. We'd been divorced over two years before my symptoms indicated I'd eventually have to undergo an operation."

Her mom leaned forward. "Even more reason why you should let Raoul know your situation the next time you're with him. He's fallen for you."

"What if he freaks out too?"

"Raoul Fontesquieu is a strong man who won't fall apart. But if you don't tell him and he finds out you held back, then he might not trust you. That could doom your relationship."

"I'm already doomed."

Her mother scoffed.

"Maman—have you forgotten I have to get through the operation? We don't know if I'll be able to live a full life or take that job at Gaillard's. I might not even leave the hospital," her voice faded.

"Nonsense. I know you're going to be fine."

"No—you *don't* know! None of us, not even the doctor can predict what will happen."

"That's true," she came back. "But the thought of losing my precious daughter is something I refuse to consider. So please do me this favor and tell him the truth soon."

On Wednesday morning, Raoul woke up to play with his son, relieved that Cami would be coming to the villa this evening. Last Saturday while she'd worked alongside him, Raoul had found himself enamored of her. It was no longer just a physical attraction.

In meeting Cami, he'd started to come alive again. As he'd told her, he'd been developing a new consulting business to do with wine not connected with Fontesquieu. Raoul knew his father was enraged over the divorce and for his noncompliance as CEO, but that didn't worry him.

Now that he'd cut himself off from the family business, Raoul already had his own resources to do something that would bring income and a sense of pride over what his great uncle—a scientist, vine culture expert and artist—had envisioned years before. He wanted to build this into a legacy for Alain.

Cami not only applauded his ideas, she'd assured him his son would follow him anywhere. Just remembering what she'd said put a smile on his face. To envision her driving around Vence in her own taxi came close to giving him a heart attack. Her engaging personality was like no one else's.

Feelings and desires that had been buried for the last few years had come back. His mind told him he wasn't practicing enough caution with Cami, but at this point his heart was driving him and trumped everything else.

Frustrated that she wouldn't be coming to the villa anymore to work, he'd asked her out to dinner last night so he could express his feelings. To his joy she'd agreed to come swimming. Tonight, he would open up his heart to her.

At five, he went upstairs to shower and shave. Cami would be arriving any minute. Alain was in the playroom with Nathalie. He came back down to the kitchen. Through the window he saw her Citroën approach.

His pulse went into high gear. He loved her hair flowing, but once again her lustrous black tresses had been caught back in a chignon. She got out wearing another pair of jeans and an ivory-colored pullover that revealed her lovely shape. He opened the back door to let her in.

She entered and looked around. The room was cluttered with boxes full of all the things needed to supply a functioning kitchen. They needed to be opened.

Through her black lashes those hyacinth eyes met his. "What's all this?"

"Nathalie and Arlette picked out all these items at the store. It needs to be sorted and put away. I'll get around to it when I have time, but I'm afraid that living at the château all my life didn't teach me to deal with these logistics."

She smiled. "The fact that you were asked to be CEO proves your talents were better spent outside the kitchen."

"I guess we'll never know. The coffee's hot. I've poured you a mug."

"Thank you."

"Just give me a moment and I'll be right back."

Cami had to pinch herself to believe she was here again when she'd thought she'd seen the last of him. While she was sipping the hot liquid, she heard footsteps. Suddenly Raoul entered the kitchen with the cutest little boy she'd ever seen in her life.

With curly black hair and a lean build, his son Alain couldn't belong to any other man and would grow up to be impossibly handsome like his striking father. Both were in jeans and T-shirts. Alain wore a light blue one with a bulldog on the front.

Raoul flashed her a smile and hunkered down by him. "Alain, this is Cami."

Her heart melted as she leaned toward him and smiled. Talk about the perfect child! What she would have given for a son like this, but not when she'd been in a bad marriage.

"Bonjour, Alain—" *You darling boy.* Obeying an impulse, she touched the dog on his shirt. "I like your *chien.*"

He didn't hide from her. Instead he stood very still, staring at her through piercing black eyes exactly like his father's.

"I'm planning to get him a bulldog as soon as I can find the right nanny and she gets settled in. We'll all train it together."

"They're a lot of work, but they're wonderful."

"I wanted one all my life, but there was a no pets rule while I was growing up."

"Really? More than once I heard my father say a child needed a dog."

"Not all parents feel the same way."

She frowned. "That's no fun, Raoul. We had two dogs while I was growing up. I'd get home from school and play with them for hours."

He smiled. "Lucky you."

"I know I was, especially because I didn't have any siblings. When the last one died, we didn't get another one because by then I was married. Then after the divorce, I started working with my mom. We didn't get a new dog because we couldn't give it the attention it deserves."

"That's not going to be our problem around here," Raoul murmured.

"A boy and his dog. Could anything be cuter?" She reached for her purse on the counter and pulled out the little present she'd bought for his son at a toy store on the way here. "You were so excited about Alain coming home to live with you, I wanted to get this for him in celebration. This is for your nursery collection." Cami had noticed he didn't have a white toy car.

Raoul's eyes thanked her as he took it from her and unwrapped it. "Look, Alain. A white Porsche Cabriolet. You couldn't have bought him anything more exciting."

Alain's attention fastened on the car before reaching for it. In the next instant he got down on the floor with it and started pushing it around making funny sounds she was sure his father had taught him. That brought laughter from both of them.

"I can tell you've already been teaching him the important things of life, Raoul." His eyes met hers in amusement, causing her heart to beat faster. "I don't know what it is about men. They all love sports cars. I have to admit I love them too." But she'd never had the fun of driving in one. Her friends and acquaintances couldn't afford them.

His burning black eyes played over her, sending sensations of warmth through her body. "I'm hoping he'll love to swim too. I'm giving him his first lesson in our indoor swimming pool."

"Are you sure you want anyone else there while you're teaching him?"

He cocked his dark head. "I'm thinking if he sees someone else swimming, it will give him courage."

"That's a thought, but I'm only an average swimmer." The doctor hadn't told her to curtail her normal activities, but he'd cautioned her not to overdo. As well as instructing she should do no heavy lifting or running marathons, he'd said she shouldn't take part in swimming meets either.

An enticing smile broke the corner of his mouth. "All it takes is a little practice."

"I'm sure that's true." This could be the last time she ever went swimming in her life, let alone with this man she adored. Raoul had to be the most eligible, hunky male on the planet. "How about I just dangle my legs over the edge of the pool."

Raoul's eyes flickered. "You won't get any complaints from me."

Why did she have to say that?

"After our swim we'll have a meal in the kitchen that you and your coworkers have made shine."

She hadn't been imagining it. Last night Raoul had told her he wanted to be with her all the time, but it could be a very short-lived relationship. It all depended on the result of the operation.

"Come upstairs with us first and I'll get him changed. Then we'll go down. We want company, don't we, *mon gars*?"

It was crazy, but there was nothing in the world she wanted more than to be with him like this. "Let's go."

When they reached the nursery, Raoul put the Porsche on the dresser and pulled a little swimsuit out of the drawer with baby sharks on it.

Cami chuckled. "Did you buy this?"

There was a glint in his eyes. "I couldn't

resist." He lowered Alain in the crib and put a clean diaper on him like he'd been doing it forever, then followed with the suit. Alain kept staring at her.

"I'll take him to my bedroom while I change. You would know there's a bathroom off the hall with towels outside the indoor pool. You can change in there and we'll meet at the pool."

She hurried off with a throbbing pulse and discovered the luxurious bathroom that now contained every amenity and a supply of beach towels. Someone had been busy adding all the furnishings. Cami removed her jeans and blouse. She's brought her modest blue bikini.

On her way out the door she reached for three towels and went to the pool.

Raoul had beaten her there and was pushing his son around on a blue inflatable raft. Fully clothed or in a swimsuit, he had to be the most exciting-looking male alive with a dusting of black hair on his chest.

She felt those matching black eyes appraise her as she walked to the shallow end. After putting the towels on a deck chair, she sat on the top step of the pool.

Alain saw her and pointed. "That's Cami," his father said. "Can you say Cami?"

"Cam—" he blurted to her delight.

"That's right, Alain," she cried. "I bet you're having fun with your papa." Her gaze darted to Raoul's. "Has he ever been swimming?"

He pulled Alain off the raft and moved closer. "Nathalie took him to a pool a couple of times during the summer, but that's the sum total of his experience."

She noticed how tender he was with his son, swishing him around in the water at the shallow end without alarming him. In a minute she slipped in the warm water and swam by them. Raoul urged him to kick his legs. Cami stretched out alongside and kicked her legs too. Pretty soon Alain got so excited Raoul's laughter resounded in the pool room.

She swam over to them. "Shall we watch your papa?" Cami instinctively reached for Alain.

CHAPTER SIX

RAOUL WAS EXCITED to see that his son went to her willingly and didn't cry for him.

"Let's see how big a splash *he* can make," she said to him.

Raoul sent her a smile before he starting swimming on his back. His legs and feet created a geyser that fascinated her and Alain. "Papa—"

"That's right, Alain. Your papa didn't tell us he was an Olympic champion!"

More laughter escaped Raoul's lips. It was all too fun. In another minute he joined them and put Alain through another series of kicking exercises. She swam to the raft and pushed it over to Raoul. He lifted Alain onto it so he could move him around again.

She followed them while Raoul made figure eights and circles. Alain was loving it. So was he. In fact this was the most fun he'd had in ages.

"You really are an amazing swimmer. Did the château have a swimming pool?"

"No. I wish there'd been one. On occasion I was allowed to swim on the estate of a friend my family approved of. In my midteens Dominic and I swam in the ocean when we finished our vineyard work. That's another reason I bought this villa. My son is going to be able to swim whenever he wants."

"He's taking to it already."

Raoul pushed Alain on the raft toward her. "I want him to love his life growing up. I wasn't as happy at home or at school."

Cami pushed Alain back to him, causing him to laugh. "Why didn't you like school? I love hearing about your life."

"You already know a lot. The private school I attended was structured the way my grandfather ran everything."

"In other words, you didn't get a break."

"Not until college."

"Where did you go?"

"I went to the Institute of Vine and Wine Science in Bordeaux."

"Bordeaux? So you really got away from here. How did you manage that?"

He smiled. "Jerome's wife, Danie, was born in Bordeaux. Decades ago Jerome went to a wine conference there and happened to visit her family's vineyard. The two met and married. In time she inherited a small château. They visited it once in a while.

"When I turned eighteen, they prevailed on my grandfather and father to let me go live with them while I studied at the institute. It was understood we'd all be back to live at the château and I would work for the family. Living with them during that time was one of the happier periods of my life."

"So the Degardelle name comes from her side of the family."

"Your mind doesn't forget a thing, does it? Yes, that was one of her family names that goes way back. I'd love to tell you more, but Alain is starting to fuss and it's time to go in. We've been out here long enough and he's hungry. I think we all are. I'll meet you in the kitchen and feed him before putting him down."

He watched her hurry out of the pool and wrap a towel around her beautiful body before she disappeared.

"Alain must have gone down easily," Cami said as Raoul came in the kitchen soon after.

"Yes. He ate fast and all the exercise wore him out." A minute later he'd put salad and sandwiches on the table and joined her.

"He's wonderful, Raoul, and so well behaved I'm impressed." Cami started eating.

"That's Arlette's and Minerve's doing."

"If you can't find the right nanny, would this Minerve agree to go on doing it?"

"No. She lives with her family in La Gaude. I'm in the process of looking for one who lives in Vence."

She sat back in the chair. "Since she's been with Alain from the beginning, that's not going to be easy."

Raoul shook his head. "I've already interviewed five candidates, but no one seems right yet. Especially not the last one." They both smiled in understanding. He finished one sandwich and started a second one.

"It must be difficult to trust another person to take care of your son. I don't envy you."

He focused his attention on her. "I haven't thanked you for the Porsche you gave Alain. As you noticed, he loved it."

"He was so cute. What I could see was the bond you two have. I'm happy for you. It won't be long before he's swimming circles around you. Now I have to leave."

"I know you have work tomorrow. Cami? Do you ever want to do anything else that isn't so physically demanding all the time?"

"Why do you ask?"

Raoul thought she'd paled a little and noticed the troubled look that crossed over her features. "I'm sorry if I offended you, Cami. It's just that you work so hard every day, it seems like you rarely get a break. But I didn't mean to impl—"

"You didn't offend me," she broke in. "You would never do that. It's just that your question surprised me because I'll actually be starting a new job after the holidays."

"What do you mean *new*? Is it with a different cleaning company?"

"No. I'll be working in the finance department at La Maison de Chocolat Gaillard."

Gaillard? It was probably the biggest historic candy company in Southern France with headquarters in Nice. One of their branches was here in Vence. Fabrice Gaillard, the CEO, was a friend of Raoul's father. They were the same kind of formidable men who belonged to the same exclusive bridge club only a few elites were permitted to join.

He sat forward. "Now you've got me mystified."

A smile broke out on her lovely face. "Let me start at the beginning so you can understand how I got into cleaning. After my pathetic ten-month marriage, I divorced my husband."

"You said it was over fast."

"I should never have married him. We met while we were both in a play in high school for our drama class. It was a watered-down version of *Le Vicomte de Bragelonne*, better known as *The Man in the Iron Mask*. I played a maid and Christophe took the role of a groom of one of the Musketeers."

"The Dumas tales are some of my favorites," Raoul interjected.

"Mine too. We had a lot of fun and performed for four nights. Between the costumes and all the makeup, it was very exciting. He was cute and loaded with personality. Everyone liked him, especially the girls.

"After it was over, we started seeing each other until we became inseparable. He brought excitement into my life and I was convinced I'd fallen in love. We wanted to get married." She flicked Raoul a glance. "Big mistake."

Raoul eyed her intently. "Why didn't it work?"

"Naively, I thought he wanted a real marriage. I intended to be the best wife possible. We got married midsummer and moved in with his parents. He had a Vespa and we got around on that until we could afford to buy a car. He was an only child. They had room at their house and insisted we live with them until we got on our feet."

"You liked them?"

"Yes, but by the end of our first month I was unhappy."

He squinted. "Only a month?"

She nodded. "By then I knew our marriage was never meant to be. He'd lost his job at a car body shop. I found out later he'd been going in late and not finishing his work. He was a child who liked to play too much. Christophe wanted things, but he didn't have the money to pay for them."

"How did you manage?"

"I got a job at a *librairie* and sold books."

His brows went up. "So it was *you* who brought home the paycheck."

"Yes, and his parents provided a home for us. He applied for another job at an *epicier* and kept it for a while. But one night he came home drunk, and confessed he'd lost that job. I found out later he'd gotten involved with a girl who worked there."

Her story was a terribly sad one. "I'm *desolé* for you, Cami."

"Things went from bad to worse. When I found out he'd been with another girl and couldn't hold on to his next job, that was it. We weren't going to make it. Thankfully I hadn't gotten pregnant and couldn't believe I'd gotten myself into such a bad situation.

He had no desire to go to college or learn a trade. I told him I wanted a divorce."

"How did that go over?"

"He took off. That was his way when he couldn't cope. Of course he always came back to his parents when he ran out of money. At that point I didn't care and went to court to obtain a divorce with the money I'd earned at the bookstore. Then I moved back in with Maman."

"How could he have let you go? I can't comprehend it." Raoul couldn't imagine it. "Didn't he try to fight you on it?"

"Not Christophe." She started to say something else, then held back. There was still something she wasn't telling him. He had an idea it was important. Cami had sounded far away from him just now. Raoul knew a serious issue of some kind was going on inside of her that had nothing to do with her disastrous marriage seven years ago.

"We've talked about your divorce, but I didn't ask if there's someone else in your life now." He didn't really believe it, not after the way she'd returned his kisses, but he had to ask.

"More like some*thing* else."

"You mean your new job."

After a slight hesitation he heard her say, "Yes. I intend to succeed."

Again Raoul had the impression there was more she wasn't telling him. Before long he intended to find out what it was.

"As we both found out, not all marriages are happy ones, Cami."

"You're right. I quit my job and started going to work with Maman cleaning houses. That's how my cleaning career got started. The pay was so much better and paid the insurance. When I'd saved enough money to pay for the first semester, I enrolled in business and finance at Sophie Antipolis University in Nice."

His thoughts reeled. "That means you had to be a top student in high school."

"My high school English teacher encouraged me to work hard and apply for a scholarship."

"And you got it."

She nodded. Cami's modesty was another quality he admired about her. After their first meeting, she hadn't come on to him at all, or try to impress him. Nothing flirtatious. Just the opposite in fact. That quality made him want her more and intrigued him.

"I told you my father was a taxi driver. He suffered from the fact that neither he nor my mother ever went to college. Both of them impressed upon me the need to get good grades and attend university since neither of their families had ever gone for higher education."

"Your mother must be so proud, but I'm sorry your father still isn't alive to see what you've accomplished."

"Me too. Anyway, I matriculated and commuted by bus. I'd work with Maman for one semester to earn money, then attend the university for one semester. I told you our boss at NI was terrific. She let me work when I could. After seven years, I've taken my last exams and graduated mid-November."

Raoul sat there in shock. The patience and determination she'd displayed to get to this point made her outstanding in his eyes. "You didn't just get a job there. It means you must have graduated with highest honors."

She brushed it off. "What matters now is to prove myself. I was an intern there for the last semester and will be working in the same accounting department as before."

"Even those intern jobs are handpicked." He shook his head. "The way I've seen you work around here has been a revelation. I have no doubts they'll be thankful they hired you."

"Thank you, Raoul. Give me ten years and we'll see if all that schooling was worth it. Now I'm afraid I really have to go." She got up from the table. "Thank you for everything."

"I don't want you to leave." Raoul followed her out to the car. "You look so beautiful out here with the light shining from the window." He kissed her hungrily and heard her moan of desire, igniting his passion. "I don't know how I'm going to let you drive away, but I realize I have to."

"The last thing I want to do is leave, Raoul." They kissed again, both of them breathless before she got in the car.

"Your presence in the pool made a difference with Alain."

"It was so much fun with him."

"I know he enjoyed you. We'll do it again soon. As for tomorrow evening, will you let me pick you up around five thirty or six? We'll have dinner and drive around to see the sound and light show in Vence. The car will keep us warm."

"That sounds fabulous."

He kissed her once more and shut the door before waving her off.

Raoul was in a daze when he walked in the villa. She was a college graduate with honors and would be starting to work at Gaillard's in January. She'd worked so hard for everything all her life. What an incredible woman. Tomorrow night he wanted to do something special to surprise and honor her. For that to happen, he needed to make a certain phone call.

On Thursday evening Cami and her mom returned to the apartment after work and she got ready to go out with Raoul. Her thoughts were focused on his life that had been so different than she had imagined.

Being with him made her long to be with him all the time, which was an impossibility if she didn't have a clean bill of health.

That's what was troubling about daring to dream.

"*Non*, Maman," she said before her mother could ask her if she'd told the truth to Raoul. "But I'll tell him soon." With that promise, she hurried to shower and get ready.

She knew her mom was right, especially after the scare she'd had last evening when Raoul had asked her about continuing with her cleaning career. For a moment she'd feared he'd somehow figured out something was wrong with her physically.

Cami couldn't put it off any longer, but wondered if her parent was being too optimistic about the success of the operation. Cami might not have a good recovery and wouldn't be able to take the position at Gaillard's after all.

She might turn into an invalid with a shorter life span. How would Raoul feel about that? What if Cami was one of the small percentage that died during the procedure? Not everyone survived a heart operation, even if they'd been in excellent health otherwise.

She'd read stories on the internet that

had frightened her. In the dark hours of the night she'd sometimes wake up in a cold sweat worrying that something could go wrong. The doctor had advised her not to dwell on the negative, but he wasn't the one who'd been living with this threat for the last five years.

When Raoul came to the apartment to pick her up, he was wearing a dark brown suit and lighter brown shirt without a tie. She had to discipline herself not to stare at him. "Are you ready?"

"Yes." Beneath her coat she wore a silky soft orange blouse and navy skirt. Before they reached the car he started kissing her. They must have been out there five minutes trying to become one before someone pulled in to the parking lot and he let her go.

"We're eating at Le Petit Auberge. Have you been there before?"

"No." She'd heard of it, but her budget couldn't have afforded to dine there.

"They serve the best beef kebabs. Another favorite of mine is chicken stuffed with veal and served with vegetables from their hothouse garden."

"Already my mouth is watering."

Cami felt like she was in a fantastic dream as he drove them up the mountain road. He took several winding roads that eventually brought them to the *auberge* hidden in the trees. Such an idyllic setting.

There weren't many cars, but of course the hour was early for most people to go to dinner. He parked the car and shut off the motor. "I know you're going to like this place."

"I have no doubt of it."

After helping her out, they walked inside. He cupped her elbow. He would never know how much she craved the contact. The need to touch him was growing into an ache that refused to go away.

This was no bistro. Raoul was greeted like royalty and they were shown a table, the only one with a centerpiece of pink roses. She marveled that he'd gone to all this trouble for her.

Once seated, a waiter arrived to pour the wine while another waiter brought menus and took their orders.

Raoul's eyes roamed over her, sending her heart into thud speed. "You look ravishing tonight. I decided we need to celebrate your new position at Gaillard's."

Heat filled her cheeks. "You're the most thoughtful person I've ever known."

He shook his head. "You deserve honoring. I don't think you have any idea of how phenomenal that is."

She sipped the wine. "Why do you say that?"

"Because the CEO is a close friend of my father's."

"You're kidding—"

"I happen to know that you had to pass a stringent series of tests to be hired there. They don't let just anyone work for them."

"Naturally I never met the CEO. What's he like?"

"In truth, he's ruthless like my father, and scary to approach. If he agreed to hire you, then he was impressed by your performance more than you know. Otherwise you wouldn't be working for the company." He sounded far away just then.

"I guess it's nice to hear I was offered a position there." But what he'd said about his own father and his childhood sent a shiver down Cami's spine and brought forcefully to mind his troubled relationship with the men in his family. Now that she knew so much more about his unhappy past, she could understand why he was breaking with them.

"I told you this to pay you a compliment, not to worry you."

"At least I've been forewarned."

Cami was glad the waiter came with their dinner. She'd chosen the chicken and veal. "This food is absolutely delicious. I haven't tasted anything this good in ages."

"Neither have I," he confessed.

Her thoughts raced ahead. "Have you found a new housekeeper yet?"

"No."

"Will you ask this one to cook for you?"

"Only a few meals."

"Then you'll cook the rest of the time?"

"Yes, especially when I go out on the sailboat. It's moored in Nice."

Of course he had a sailboat. While she was imagining it, he called the waiter over and ordered some takeout for her mother, then turned to her.

"Would you like dessert?"

"No, thank you. I couldn't."

Their meal was coming to an end. The drive was coming up. That's when she planned to tell him about her heart condition, but she was nervous.

"Before we leave, I have a little gift for you." He pulled it out of his breast pocket and put it on the table above her plate.

She shook her head. "No more. You've done too much already. I couldn't accept it."

"Not even to commemorate you're being taken on at Gaillard's?"

Cami took a deep breath. She assumed it was chocolate and was so small it couldn't be too expensive. She didn't want to appear impolite so she picked it up and unwrapped it. To her surprise it was a weightless, three-by-four-inch black box with a lovely purple violet on the lid and the name Gaillard printed below it. Not understanding, she lifted it.

Inside the tissue she counted twelve exquisite, individual violet heads of petals that glistened with sugar crystals. She shot him a questioning glance.

"Today Gaillard's is famous for its chocolate. What few people know is that five hundred years ago the first Gaillard concocted a recipe for sugared violets that eventually grew to other kinds of sugared flowers. They became the first candy company in Provence enjoyed by kings and queens from all over Europe before the product was discontinued and chocolate took over."

Cami was astounded.

"Since you're going to be working for them, I thought you might like to taste the first product they ever made. Your coworkers will be impressed that you have knowledge of something that isn't generally known.

"In fact, I venture to guess that no one working there today has ever eaten one. Other companies make them, but they came later and never could replicate the original. I had this especially ordered for you because it's a secret recipe and no longer available except for a select few clients who have an in with the man at the top."

Meaning Raoul himself.

Cami looked down, aware of tears stinging her eyelids. She loved him so terribly, and had already found out Raoul was an amazingly generous man. But for him to do this expressly for her in honor of her new job left her touched…speechless.

"Thank you. I—I can't wait to try one," she stammered. But the whole time that her gaze was fastened on the box of sugared violets, she was thinking about all he'd done for her and knew she'd fallen madly in love with him. But it frightened her.

Suddenly Cami couldn't handle this any longer. "Raoul—why have you done all this for me? I don't mean just the violets. I'm talking about everything since the day I came to clean for you—the flowers, the dinners out, your kindness to my mother. You must know I'm overwhelmed by all you've done."

CHAPTER SEVEN

"THEN LET ME EXPLAIN," he said in a thick-toned voice. "I'd been in hell for a long time before I found out I had a son. I've wanted to make everything perfect for him. When I saw an attractive woman up on the ladder cleaning my son's room with such care, I didn't realize I'd startled you. It would have been my fault if you'd had a bad accident.

"After you fell in my arms, I found myself staring into a pair of incredible eyes. Blame their color. You had me mesmerized. The truth is, I found myself wanting to get to know you better."

"I still don't understand why."

"I guess you'd have to be a man to understand."

"Please tell me the real truth." She refused to be put off.

One black brow lifted. "That *is* the real truth," he came back with force.

Cami sat back in the chair, appearing haunted by his remark. "How often does this kind of thing happen to you? Everything that's happening seems too good to be true."

He finished the rest of his coffee. "That's a fair question. You have every right to ask it. The answer is, it has only happened to me one other time in my life. In truth it was on the night I met Alain's mother at a bistro near the vineyard three years ago.

"She taught elementary school and had come in with friends one night. I had been checking the wine inventory and was so drawn to her from that first moment, I approached her to have a drink with me. We fell in love that night."

"But then you stopped seeing her and got married. Do I have that right?"

Raoul nodded. "Before I ever met Antoinette, my parents gave a lavish party where I was introduced to Sabine Murat. I soon discovered that her parents and mine had been plotting to arrange a marriage between us for a long time. I admit I found her attractive and intelligent, but the more I spent time with her, the more I realized the essential ingredient I needed to feel was missing."

Cami nodded. "As I told you, after a month of marriage I felt the same way, Raoul. Only I'd already taken vows."

"Understood," Raoul murmured. "Like a fool, I slept with her once. It was wrong, but I thought maybe that would change the way I felt about her. But it didn't. I wasn't in love and I broke it off with her because it wasn't fair to either of us. I'd had relationships with several women over the years, but I'd never been in love. I began to believe love was out of my reach.

"Then I met Antoinette. We spent every possible moment together and I knew I wanted to marry her as soon as we could. Before we could let her parents know, I received a call from Sabine whom I hadn't seen for over a month." He grimaced. "To my horror she told me she was expecting our baby. I couldn't believe it, knowing I'd taken precautions. But the doctor confirmed it."

"You had a *baby* with her?" A groan escaped her lips. He knew he'd shocked her. "I had no idea and can't imagine what a nightmare that must have been."

"You'll never know. I had to give up the only love of my life and marry Sabine who moved in my apartment at the château. I never saw Antoinette again, though I tried calling her to talk. She refused, knowing we couldn't have a future. It was agony.

"From that point on I concentrated on the pregnancy and birth of our little girl, Celine. She brought me my only happiness, but she was born early and died of a bad heart within the month."

"What?" The shock of hearing Raoul had a baby with Sabine was one thing, but the revelation that it had died of heart problems was almost too much for Cami to bear.

Raoul eyed her soulfully with those black eyes. "I was in despair over losing her. When I asked the doctor if the baby's heart condition was the reason for her being premature, he shook his head and said Celine had been full-term."

"I don't understand. You didn't know that?"

He took a deep breath. “I’m afraid not. Those words meant the baby *wasn’t* mine.”

“No—” Cami blurted as the truth of it sank in. “She lied to you?” He nodded. “I can’t imagine it.” Tears filled her eyes. “The pain you must have suffered.”

“Celine was someone else’s,” his voice grated, “though at the time it never occurred to me she wasn’t mine. Worse, I suffered horribly to realize no surgical procedure could save the baby. Her heart was too damaged.”

A shudder ran through Cami. Her greatest fear was that the surgeon would find that her own heart was too damaged to fix. Throughout their dinner she’d been on the verge of telling Raoul the truth about the operation coming up, but she couldn’t do that now. He’d been through too much. It would be better to go through the surgery without him knowing anything in order to spare him.

“I’m so desperately sorry for you, Raoul. I don’t know how you’ve lived through all this.”

“It wasn’t the best of times. Sabine pretended the baby was mine so I’d marry her.

She didn't love the man who'd made her pregnant."

"I don't know how she could have done that to you."

"She'd been determined to marry me from the beginning and hold on to me. I wanted to divorce her, but the psychiatrist Sabine's family had brought in told me to put it off. He explained she was so grief-stricken over the loss and burial, he advised me to wait until she'd recovered enough to deal with the breakup of our marriage.

"I waited as long as I could stand before filing. We'd lived apart for over two months. During that time I visited Celine's grave several times, but I only became a free man the day before my grandfather died."

While he'd been telling his tragic story, Cami's mind reeled. Not only had the baby been born with a heart problem like hers, Raoul wasn't the man she'd believed went through women like water whenever he needed a diversion. He hadn't had an affair on Sabine. Cami had judged him without knowing the truth.

"It was during that waiting period Sabine's family wanted us to go in for marriage counseling. She demanded more money from me if I refused, but I couldn't do it. Nothing could fix what was wrong between us when I wasn't in love with her."

"I hear what you're saying," Cami murmured. "When love dies, that's it."

"Amen," he said in a gravelly tone.

"Raoul? How did you and Alain find each other?"

He finished his coffee. "During that desolate time, Nathalie came to the vineyard looking for the stranger who had impregnated her deceased stepsister Antoinette. She posed as a grape picker and met my cousin Dominic. They fell in love, which is an amazing story in itself."

"You mean she actually helped with the harvest?"

"Yes, for several weeks. They became enamored right away. In time he found out her real reason for coming to the vineyard. It turned out she thought Dominic or his brother Etienne might be Alain's father because they all look so much alike. But neither one claimed to know Antoinette.

"Then she met me and wondered if *I*

could be the one because of the strong family resemblance."

"You and Alain are clones of each other," she cried.

"Don't I know it. We looked so much alike I was in shock. When she showed me Antoinette's picture, the puzzle was solved and I was united with the son I'd had no knowledge of. The whole thing was miraculous."

"I'll say it was," Cami murmured in amazement. "Antoinette never told her family your name?"

"No. We'd wanted to keep everything quiet until our announcement. When I had to tell her about Sabine's pregnancy, she didn't want her parents to know anything."

A groan escaped Cami's lips. "How impossible and heartbreaking for both of you."

"I'm still suffering from guilt over hurting her the way I did."

Cami's heart was pained for him. "You should let it go. Alain's grandmother seems to love you very much."

"I'm still in awe over her kindness to me."

"She has to be thrilled you're her grandson's father."

"I'm thrilled too. One look at him and I saw Antoinette in his features. It was like getting part of her back. The joy of knowing I had a son brought me alive again and I determined to be the best father possible."

"I can tell you already are," she said softly.

"Time will tell. Dominic married Nathalie and we both bought villas near each other. My life took on new meaning to plan a future around my son. Getting the villa ready, finding housecleaners so I could furnish everything meant the world to me. Now you've come into my life, I'm happier than I've ever been."

She felt the same way, but couldn't say it back. Not now. He didn't need to hear about the state of her health. In a few more days she'd be away from his world, dealing with the crisis she'd been dreading.

He wouldn't be there with her...

By now the waiter brought a bag with the food, which Raoul took. It was time to go. Cami got up and the two of them walked outside to his car. He put the bag of food in back before helping her. Again she felt his hand on her elbow. Before they got in his car, he pulled her against him and lowered his mouth to hers, kissing her possessively.

Cami moaned, relishing the taste and feel of him. She couldn't get close enough. Every touch of his hands and lips electrified her. The sensual tension between them was so strong, she knew he felt the same way.

"I was dying to kiss you like this the whole time we were inside," he admitted, then let her go because people were arriving, but there was a marked change in their relationship because she was totally in love with him.

They drove into town and looked at the illuminated buildings. At one point, he parked the car. "Shall we have our dessert now?" Raoul lifted the lid on the violets and put the box in front of her. "Are you ready to enjoy the favorite treat of royalty that kept the dentists of the time busy?"

Cami broke into laughter. She couldn't help it. "Have you ever tried one?"

"No. This will be my first time too."

He reached for one and put it in his mouth.

She followed suit and sucked on it before chewing it. "Um. It tastes like a violet smells."

"Agreed. I think I prefer chocolate." His grin delighted her.

"I can't wait to show these to Maman. I have to admit I'm curious to see if she'll try eating one. It's so odd to think of eating flowers."

"Many violets are edible and can be sautéed or steamed. Some cooks stir them into soups as a thickener."

"I had no idea." His knowledge astounded her.

"Do you know our company makes a yellow-green liqueur called Fontesquieu Chartreuse? The secret ingredient includes carnation petals among the other herbs and plants distilled."

"You're kidding—"

"Not at all. Jerome originated the recipe. It's in one of the journals and I have to get them back. One day I'll take you to the winery again and you can test it out for yourself."

"That would really be something. Imagine drinking carnations and eating violet soup. I feel like I've entered a world full of magic."

"It was Olivarri who said, 'Wine is the only artwork you can drink.'"

More laughter escaped as she studied him. "It's so much fun spending time with you, I've lost all sense of my surroundings."

"You're not the only one," he whispered and kissed her. They both tasted of violets. This evening had been heavenly, but there wouldn't be many more of them. Though she was dying inside of love for him and wanted to pour out her love, she couldn't do it. Until the operation was over, he was better off not knowing anything.

After they reached the apartment and he'd parked, she turned to him. "Thank you for tonight. I'll remember it forever."

"So will I, but it's only the beginning for us, Cami." His eyes burned like dark fires as they studied her features. Then he reached for the food and came around to her side of the car to open her door.

When they reached the apartment door, he rocked her back and forth in his arms, hugging her for a long time. She wanted to invite him in and never let him go, but she couldn't. The man had suffered too much to go through any more trauma in his life.

"Before I go, let's make plans for tomorrow evening. Alain has his checkup at the doctor's tomorrow afternoon. After we get back, I'll cook dinner for the three of us and we'll have a fun evening at home."

She eased away from him. "I have an even better idea. Tomorrow afternoon Maman and I are taking the afternoon off. I'll bring the groceries and cook dinner. It's my turn to wait on you." Cami wanted to do something special for him after all he'd done for her.

"If you mean that, nothing could make me happier," he murmured against her lips. "I'll leave the back door open for you. *À bientôt, ma belle.*"

Cami's body hummed as she entered the apartment. He'd set her on fire and she was burning up with desire. Once inside the apartment, the first thing she saw were the fabulous lavender roses, a reminder of Raoul, a man who was larger than life. She'd never forget this day for as long as she lived.

"Maman? I've brought you dinner, compliments of Le Petit Auberge."

Her mother emerged from the other room. "You mean Raoul Fontesquieu. How did he handle what you had to tell him?"

"I didn't say anything, but there's a reason. Sit down and I'll explain why."

By the time she'd explained everything about Sabine's lie, including the fact that the little baby he'd loved had died of a bad heart, her mother looked shocked and saddened.

"What a shame when you're both in love with each other. Anyone can see that. Doesn't he deserve to know what's going to happen, no matter how painful it might be for him?"

"I don't want to talk about it." She was still struggling with the pain of what the result could be following the operation. The worst result was too excruciating to contemplate. On her way to bed, she took the roses with her.

Friday morning Nathalie came to the villa to help Raoul interview a woman for the nanny position. The trim brunette Parisian widow had no children and was in her early fifties.

For three years she'd been a nanny for a diplomat's family in Paris following the death of her husband. The family no longer needed her. Since her married sister lived in Vence, she'd decided to apply for a nanny's job here to be near her only living family.

She reminded Raoul a little of Minerve, very down to earth and came with impeccable credentials. Nathalie appeared to like her too. Alain moved back and forth and played with his blocks. He didn't seem to mind a stranger being there and responded favorably to some of the things she said to him.

Raoul gave her a brief background on Alain so she'd understand this would be hard for his son to get used to a new nanny. Following a tour of the villa and an inspection of the nursery, she indicated she'd like to take care of Alain. The decision was made to hire her temporarily and see how things went. She could move into the guest room in the upstairs hall next to the nursery at any time.

Alain scuttled off Nathalie's lap and ran to him. It caught at his heart that he and his son had a special bond already. He lifted him and hugged him hard.

"He's a precious boy, Monsieur Fontesquieu."

"He is. Please call me Raoul."

"And the two of you call me Delphine." She got to her feet. "I'll leave now, and be back tomorrow."

Raoul kept Alain in his arms while he saw Delphine to the front door. "From now on, plan to park in the back. Here's the key to the back door."

"*Très bien. Au revoir*, Alain." She touched his son's cheek before leaving.

He shut the door, feeling an enormous weight lift from his heart that he'd found a woman he could work with. Though there were no guarantees, hopefully Alain would learn to like her, but it would take time.

His son squirmed to get down. Raoul lowered him to the floor and they walked back to the sitting room to find Nathalie.

She smiled at him. "I like her, Raoul. She's solid and very cute with Alain."

"I agree with you. I think it'll work with Delphine."

"I couldn't be happier for you. After you've taken Alain to the doctor, why don't you drive him to La Gaude? Mom and I will tend him. Later Dom and I will bring him back in time for bed. You don't know how much I miss him."

His sister-in-law knew he was dying to be alone with Cami. There were no secrets at this point. "You're sure?"

"Don't be an idiot. It's long past time you found someone." She gave Alain a kiss.

"Thanks, Nathalie."

"I owe you big-time after the way you helped me get back with Dominic. We're so happy it's ridiculous, and we want you to know that same feeling again." She kissed Raoul's cheek and left.

Raoul wasn't far behind with Alain to take him to the doctor. So far his son seemed perfectly healthy, but Raoul was a bit nervous. This was all part of being a new parent as Arlette had reminded him earlier. The knowledge that Cami would be arriving at the villa later to fix their dinner filled him with excitement and helped him deal with his worry over being a dad.

When Cami arrived at the villa at three, it was clear that Raoul hadn't returned from the doctor yet. He'd left the back door unlocked and she was able to walk in and get busy cooking her specialty of *escalope de veau* and roast potatoes.

She was still smiling over her mother's surprised reaction to the candied violets she ate and loved when she heard the doorbell ring. It was probably a delivery of some kind for Raoul. She wiped her hands on a towel and walked through the villa to answer the door.

A stunning auburn-haired woman probably late twenties, dressed in a designer suit stood there scrutinizing Cami who was wearing jeans and a pale yellow crewneck pullover. The woman carried two wrapped packages hanging at her sides.

"May I help you?"

"I'm here to see Raoul Fontesquieu."

"I'm afraid he's not here, but I expect him later."

"Will you see he gets these as soon as possible?"

"Of course."

She handed her the packages and left before Cami could ask the woman's name. Cami suspected she'd just met Sabine.

After she disappeared down the steps, Cami shut the door and carried them to the kitchen where she placed them on the counter. No sooner had she put their dinner in the oven than the phone rang.

It was Raoul. Her pulse raced as she clicked on. "Hi!"

"Hi, yourself. I dropped off Alain at his grandmother's and I'm driving home from La Gaude, but there's been a traffic accident. I may not be there for another ten minutes."

"That's no problem. As I've got you on the phone, you should know a woman came to the door and left two packages for you."

"Interesting. Will you do me a favor and open them?"

"All right." She walked over and undid the paper on both of them. "They're framed oil paintings of a vineyard. Oh! Your great uncle Jerome's signature is in the lower right-hand corner of both. I didn't know he was an artist too!"

"He was a Renaissance man and did them when he was in Bordeaux. I thought I'd seen the last of them. They're one of my treasures. I can't wait to see them and will be home soon."

They hung up and Cami set the table. Before long Raoul walked in the kitchen. His dark gleaming eyes found hers. He kissed her long and hard. "Something smells wonderful, *ma belle*. You didn't have to do all this."

"I wanted to, and I have to tell you how impressed I am by the way you've put your kitchen together. No more boxes."

"Nope. Alain helped."

"That I would have loved to see. Which brings me to the burning question. What's the verdict from the doctor?"

He washed his hands. "My son is in perfect condition and is taller on the chart than most children his age." She noticed him examine the paintings.

"It would be a shock if he weren't," she quipped. "Come sit down and I'll serve you." As she put a plate of food in front of him, she said, "You seem particularly happy. What else is going on?"

"A lot of things. When I was out of town before, I made my cousin Jean-Pierre the official head of Sales and Marketing at a meeting. It's an enormous relief, but more importantly, I've found a nanny for Alain."

"Really?" She served herself some food and sat down, looking excited for him. "What's she like?"

"Delphine LaVaux is older and solid as Natalie said. She was a nanny in Paris for three years. Best of all, Alain didn't act shy around her or fuss like he did with the other women."

"Sounds like a good sign. You must be ecstatic."

"It's a start. She'll be over tomorrow to spend the day with him. Things are slowly falling into place. By the way, I love this veal dinner. You're a wonderful cook."

"Thank you. It was fun to prepare with all the new kitchen equipment."

"Since Nathalie will be bringing Alain home in a few hours, I thought we'd sit in front of the fire."

"I'll do the dishes first."

"Leave everything. I'll take care of things after you go home." But while they were talking, his phone rang. He glanced at the caller ID and flashed her a frustrated look. "I have to take this call. Excuse me for a minute."

After he left the kitchen, Cami had time to clear the table and start to load the dishwasher. When he returned, he looked preoccupied. The happy expression he'd brought in to the villa was no longer in sight.

"I have to go to the office and meet Jean-Pierre. It's an emergency."

Cami's heart sank. "I totally understand."

"There's no one like you." He brushed his mouth against hers. "I'll walk you out to your car. You have no idea how sorry I am, but I'll make it up to you. Since tomorrow is Saturday, I want to spend the whole day with you. I'll call you later tonight to make plans."

A whole day with Raoul? Nothing could sound more divine, but it disturbed Cami to see he was upset right now though he tried to hide it. He helped her on with her coat and walked her out to the Citroën.

"Drive home safely, *mon amour.* I couldn't bear it if anything happened to you."

His words and endearment haunted her all the way home.

It had never occurred to Cami that in cleaning other people's houses, she'd meet Raoul Fontesquieu, a man who had the power to make all other men melt into insignificance.

The results of her heart operation would determine if she ever saw him again. It frightened her that she could finally count in hours how long it would be before she checked into the hospital. Right now she couldn't comprehend life without him.

CHAPTER EIGHT

ON HIS WAY to the office at the vineyard, the conversation with Jean-Pierre went through Raoul's mind. Something was wrong. His cousin wanted help dealing with the Frères Oliviers in Aix, but that didn't make sense. They'd come to the meeting in Fréjus and there'd been no trouble. To Raoul's dismay he heard a trace of panic in his cousin's voice and knew he needed to get to the bottom of it.

The call couldn't have come at a worse moment. He'd needed time with Cami tonight, but it would have to wait until tomorrow. To walk out on her after the marvelous dinner she'd made crushed him, but it couldn't be helped.

When he arrived at his old office and walked inside, it was his graying father who was waiting for him. Heavy lines marked his face.

Today had been full of surprises! First Sabine. Now his father.

There was no sign of Jean-Pierre, which meant this meeting had been concocted to force the inevitable confrontation. Poor Jean-Pierre who now had to function under Raoul's father.

At last the moment had come Raoul had been waiting for. He was ready.

His tall, thin parent stood there on the verge of exploding. "What do you mean putting Jean-Pierre officially in charge?"

"My cousin is perfect for the position and has earned it. I told you the day Gran'pere died that I didn't want the CEO position, nor would I continue to be the head of Marketing and Sales. I've quit."

For once Raoul knew he'd shocked him, and took advantage of the silence.

"Since I've developed my own company, I've resigned my position and have separated myself completely from our family business.

"By now you should have received my official resignation in an email. I sent it before I left for Fréjus. I expect you to correct the announcement you made to the media. If you don't, it will bring you more headaches, not me."

His father's cheeks went a ruddy color. "Sabine told me she met your illicit lover earlier today. I'd hoped that news was a piece of fiction."

Raoul knew it. Sabine's visit to the villa where she'd met Cami had ignited his father's wrath to the exploding point. It made sense this was confrontation was happening now.

"Knowing how you feel about me, let's agree it's much better I've separated myself from the company and will follow my own path from now on."

Lines broke out on his austere features. "What about Sabine and the child you lost?"

Raoul refused to go there or expose her lie. "Celine will always have a place in my heart, but my divorce is past history. We were never suited. It's another fact you need to make clear to the media. I'm building a new life."

"With your mistress and bastard son?"

Raoul wasn't surprised his father knew

about Alain, but he wasn't going to explain about Antoinette or Cami.

"You mean Alain Fontesquieu? Has your source also learned that Alain's other grandfather died several years ago? But Alain still has a living grandfather in his *gran'pere* Matthieu Fontesquieu. If you ever want to visit and get to know your grandson, you're welcome at the villa. Is there anything else? If not, I'm leaving."

He started for the door but his father followed him. His hands had formed fists at his side. "You're going to give up everything?" he bit out incredulously.

"If you mean money, I already have, and never took a sou of Sabine's. But I *am* a Fontesquieu. You don't give up your heritage, and I've had a good life to this point, but times are changing. I'm embracing those changes to make new memories and would hope you and Maman are a part of them. That's up to you."

With nothing more to say, Raoul turned on his heel and walked out of the office, leaving his stunned father to his own devices. For the first time in his life, Raoul actually sensed a crack in his papa's demeanor.

After getting in the car, he was so relieved to have thrown off the yoke that had bound him, he felt liberated and wanted to be with Cami. Unfortunately she wasn't available, so he hurried home. Nathalie would be arriving with Alain. Raoul wanted to put him to bed. Then he'd phone the woman he adored.

After Cami got back to the apartment, she found her mom talking to her aunt and uncle on the speakerphone. They were making plans for next week after Cami's operation was over.

Not wanting to think about it, she hurried into the bedroom and got ready for bed. While she was brushing her teeth, her cell rang. She jumped and picked up after the first ring.

"Raoul?"

"I'm glad you answered so fast. I've needed to hear your voice."

"Are you all right?"

"I'm fine, but I have news we need to talk about. Tonight it was my father, not Jean-Pierre, who was waiting for me. We had the confrontation predestined for a lifetime, and I officially resigned from the company."

A gasp escaped. "Was it terrible?"

"No. I'm rid of a great burden, but I won't bother you about it right now. What I'm asking is that you go sailing with me tomorrow. We'll have the whole Saturday to ourselves."

Thrilled, she clutched the counter with one hand. "What about Alain?"

"Delphine will be here. They need time together and I have to get away. Please come. There's a lot I want to talk to you about. By tomorrow the whole family will have heard this news. The reaction will be ugly. Sabine told my father about her visit and seeing you at the door. He was upset by that news.

"I'm hoping this doesn't touch you in any way, but I can't promise that it won't, or show up in the news. We need to discuss it, but not here. I'll pick you up at eight if that's all right."

"Eight is fine. *Bonne nuit*, Raoul."

Saturday turned out to be cold, but not freezing. An hour after leaving Vence, Cami and Raoul reached the port in Nice beneath a semisunny sky. They bought some food at a Chinese bistro, then Raoul drove them to the dock where they boarded his thirty-eight-foot state-of-the-art sailboat.

He helped Cami on board and handed her a life jacket to put on. Soon they went downstairs to the living area that included the captain's console. Above and below it was luxury personified. Within a few minutes the air was toasty and comfortable.

Raoul had given her startling news over the phone last night. He'd hinted at repercussions that could reach the media. Since his divorce she knew he didn't put anything past his family.

No one was kidding anybody. A new nightmare could be starting. She didn't want to be any part of it, but recognized she'd needed to come with him today so they could talk.

Raoul undid the ropes and started the motor to edge them out to the bay beyond the buoys. Through the windows belowdecks she had a spectacular view of the Mediterranean. A few boats skimmed the calm, dark blue water.

He drove ten minutes, then lowered the anchor. Once he'd pulled some drinks from the mini fridge, he walked over to the sculptured couch that ran the length of one side of the room to join her. He handed her a can of soda and sat on a chair opposite her.

"Thank you for coming with me. I wanted you to hear the whole truth from me in case something comes up during the days ahead that could worry you while you're on vacation."

Cami couldn't stand it any longer. "Was it hard telling your father?" Heavens—how could it not be? Her heart ached for him. Though he and his parent had never gotten along, there had to be love deep down.

"Your compassion is extraordinary, but the truth is, I've wanted to break with my father since my preteens."

She winced. "You're serious."

"Afraid so. I fought his demands for as long as I can remember. There's no flexibility in him, no room for another avenue of thought. He was a virtual taskmaster who expected total obedience.

"When I was ten, he did something I

couldn't forgive. I kept a hamster in my bedroom. Jerome secretly bought it for me and taught me how to take care of it. My father didn't allow animals of any kind. One day after school I found it dead and asked the maid what she knew about it. She was on my side and said my father had been in there earlier. From that day on I made preparations to run away from home."

Cami couldn't prevent tears trickling out of her eyes. His father's cruelty shook her to the foundations. "Where did you go?"

"I borrowed a friend's sleeping bag and stashed a lot of food on the top floor of the Tour de l'Est."

She leaned forward. "What is that?"

"A massive round tower on the property I've been wanting to show you. Alain would love it. The land itself was deeded to our family and contains battlements from the fifteenth century.

"Years ago someone cleared out the old weapons and munitions from the east tower. Now its eight-foot-thick walls with rooms on four floors are used to store wine. During those days I was in hiding,

I'd fill my thermos with water from the main floor sink when the guard did rounds outside."

"I can't believe it. How long were you gone?"

"Ten days."

"Oh, Raoul. Your parents must have been terrified something horrible had happened to you."

"They called the police who looked for me, but they didn't find me. It was Jerome who figured out where I might be hiding. He was the one who'd shown me around the Tour when I was younger. Sure enough he came one night when the guard was patrolling the perimeter and called out to me. He talked me into going back to the château with him. Of course, it wasn't hard to coax me."

She smiled. "You ran out of food, right?"

He chuckled. "That, plus I admit I was happy to see him. He was always kind and told me I had to let my parents know I was safe. He backed me up and talked my father out of punishing me. Jerome knew what had happened to the hamster and understood how I felt. He counseled me that when I turned eighteen, I could go away legally if that was what I wanted."

Cami stirred in place. "Why didn't you take his advice?"

"I wanted to. In fact I would have joined Dominic in Paris. He broke with his father when he turned eighteen. I was a year younger and would have gone to Paris after my eighteenth birthday. But by then Jerome was diagnosed with lung cancer."

"Oh, no—"

"He swore me to secrecy and didn't even tell his wife. Because he was a scientist, he handled his health care in his own way and turned to alternative medicine."

She couldn't believe what she was hearing. "What did he do exactly?"

"Jerome used holistic interventions of supplements, herbs, enzymes. He changed his diet and he prayed. Knowing he would eventually die, I couldn't leave him because I loved him too much. Unfortunately I couldn't even tell Dominic until the other day when we went shopping."

She let out a moan. "So you're saying your cousin had struggles with *his* father too. How heartbreaking."

Raoul nodded. "Our fathers are clones of each other and pretty impossible. The reason Dominic took off to Paris was because his relationship with his father was so toxic. He worked at different jobs and put himself through college. Afterward he got in with a prestigious investment firm and became wealthy in his own right."

"That's incredible. You and your cousin are both alike."

"Hardly. He stayed in Paris until last year."

"That long?"

"Yes. Of course he came home for major events and vacations, but never to live. Then my aunt begged him to return because my uncle was ill with pneumonia and they thought he might die. So Dominic took over the funds department in the family until my uncle recovered and was made vice president of the company. I begged Dominic to stay on, which he did."

She pressed a hand to her throat. "And *you* remained all these years because of Jerome."

"Yes. After he died, I vowed to leave the family business altogether, but I had to make sure I could support myself when the time came. Jerome had talked to me about his many business ideas and what he'd do if he were only forty years younger. His ideas became mine and I began to see light at the end of the tunnel. But by then my life had turned upside down."

"Because of the phone call from Sabine," she murmured.

Raoul suddenly stood up. "That's all in the past. Last night I told my father I was building a new life and memories. If he wants to be a part of Alain's life, he's welcome at the villa."

Cami stared at the wonderful man who could still find forgiveness inside his soul. She adored Raoul. "What did your father say?"

"It stunned him when I told him I'd resigned. There was nothing more to say and I left the office."

"I take it he didn't run after you."

"That'll be the day."

Cami might have lost her father early, but she'd always known she was loved to death. She hurt for Raoul who would never know that feeling. His father didn't deserve him. "I'm glad you've told me what happened. It's better to be forewarned."

She didn't know what the future would hold, but at least she knew he'd be happy at home with his son and running his new business. No one could have fought harder through his agony for what he wanted. If his father did anything to bring him more pain, she couldn't bear it.

For once in her life, she couldn't follow her mother's advice. There was no way she could tell him about her heart condition now. He was building a new life and didn't need anything else to worry about. As she'd once told her mother, his life was full of heartbreaks. The last thing she'd want to do was add to them.

Raoul glanced at the woman he loved. It always helped when he talked to her. Cami looked beautiful in a soft peach-toned sweater and jeans. Today she'd worn her hair back with a clip. It made him want to undo it and run his fingers through its glossy blackness again. But he'd do it later after they'd talked.

Raoul walked over to the open kitchen

area and made coffee before putting it on the table. "I hope you're hungry because I am. Shall we eat?"

"That sounds good."

After pouring the steaming brew into mugs, he put out the cartons of Chinese food. They started eating before he handed her a fortune cookie, which she opened.

"A big event is going to change your life," she read aloud. "What does yours say?"

He smiled at her before opening his. "First comes the rain before you can expect sunshine. I don't know if I like the sound of that."

"I agree neither fortune is very reassuring."

"Let's forget them. I want to talk about a week from Saturday."

Her gaze flew to his. "What's so important about it?"

His black eyes impaled her. "Dominic and Nathalie have invited us to a party. They want us to spend an evening with them."

She bit her lip. "That's sounds lovely, but by then I'll be on vacation with my mother."

He stopped chewing. "I realize that, but you won't be away from Vence, will you?"

"No, but I'll be busy."

"The whole time?"

"Yes."

Raoul put down his fork and reached for her hand. "What's going on with you, Cami? Don't tell me it's nothing. I've been around you long enough to know something is wrong. Why are you putting me off when you know I'm dying to be with you day and night?

"The only reason I haven't tried to make love to you is because you've been in my employ. But that's over and now that you're going to be on vacation, there's no reason why we can't be together all the time. I know in my heart you wouldn't be with me if you didn't feel the same way I do. Surely you realize by now that I want to marry you."

She eased her hand away, refusing to look at him. "You couldn't possibly mean that."

"You think I don't? Trust me. I fell for you the first day we met. Don't tell me it's too soon. I know what I feel. Sometimes love happens at first sight and it happened to us. You can't deny it."

"There is no us. There *can't be*." She jumped up from the table and moved over to the couch.

He followed and sank down, sliding his arm around her shoulders. "What do you mean there *can't* be? There's something you're not telling me. You've been elusive from that first amazing day. I've been waiting for you to tell me how you feel, but you've held back. I've spilled my guts to you, but maybe that isn't enough. Is it because I have a son?"

"How can you ask me that?" she cried out. Her cheeks had gone hot with color. "I've loved every minute he's been with us. He's the most precious thing on earth!"

"Then what am I missing here?"

She lowered her head. "You and I come from different worlds. You're the son of a duke and a duchess. I'm the daughter of a taxi driver and a cleaning lady."

"Come on, Cami," he bit out. "Don't pull that nonsense on me. The ridiculous business about people being born on the wrong side of the tracks has always been absurd, and I don't buy it for a second. That's not honest. I want the truth from you. If you only knew how I felt about you."

Without conscious thought he put his hands on her upper arms and heard a cry escape her lips. She fought him, but he refused to let her go and pulled her against his chest.

"I've been desperate to get close to you. That first week I used work as the only ploy I could think of to keep us together. It couldn't be any surprise that I've fallen deeply in love with you."

Her body was trembling. "You don't know what you're saying."

"Then why have I been in agony every time you've had to leave and go home? You have no idea what I went through when I had to leave town. It was pure torture for me not to be able to see your exquisite face and hold you in my arms."

"Don't say anything else."

"I can't help it." He turned her so she would look at him. "You're all I can think about, and I know you have the same problem. When I caught you in my arms that first day, we both recognized something glorious had happened. After Antoinette, the last thing I ever expected was to fall in love again, but I did."

"Y-You don't know what you're talking about." The words came out halted.

"Oh, but I do." He slid his hands to her flaming cheeks. "Before we do anything else, I'm dying to kiss you. Don't deny me what I've longed for."

He lowered his head, needing her kiss like he needed air to breathe. After moaning in protest, the mouth he'd been craving to taste again finally opened to the pressure of his. Her response electrified him and they clung to each other. He'd been wanting this for so long.

No kiss could satisfy him. It wasn't long enough or deep enough. Raoul never wanted it to end. Their hunger for each other caused him to lose track of everything but loving this divine woman who'd come into his life. He hadn't expected to feel love like this again, not after what he'd been through.

"You're so beautiful, and I love you so much. Marry me, Cami, just as soon as it's possible," he whispered, covering her face and throat with kisses. "We belong together and need each other desperately."

"Raoul—" she cried, but he smothered the sound and pulled her down on top of him.

"Let me love you, *mon tresor.* I almost died when I had to leave you last night to go to the office. Don't put me off now."

For a while longer they tried to appease their longing for each other. But far too soon his ecstasy was cut off when she pulled away from him and raced to the kitchen area.

He hurried after her, but she'd backed up against the counter. "Please don't touch me again. We can't do this, Raoul. *I* can't. I stopped believing in love a long time ago. Let's agree that we've found ourselves attracted and vulnerable, nothing more, but it mustn't go on."

"Cami—" He was frustrated out of his mind.

"I mean it, Raoul. I treasure the time I've spent with you and Alain and all the wonderful things you've done for me, but it has to be over."

"*Has* to be over? *Can't? Mustn't?* You're not making sense!"

"Please will you take us back," she begged him. Tears poured from her eyes. He'd never seen her like this before. Something was terrifying her, but he couldn't get answers from her right now. She'd closed up on him for the time being.

"I'll take us back, but you have to promise me you'll come to the villa tomorrow. It's a special day, Jerome's birthday in fact. I want to honor his memory at the cemetery and would like to take you and Alain with me. If you'll come at noon, I'll fix lunch and we'll leave."

She swallowed hard. "If I come, will you promise not to press me about marriage?"

"I didn't realize how much your divorce still pains you," his voice grated. Why hadn't she told him everything? "But yes, I promise."

In deep pain, he reluctantly let her go and walked forward to the console. After raising the anchor, he drove the boat back to port. When he pulled in the slip, he turned to see her tear-splotched face. "This isn't the end, Cami. I can promise you that."

She refused to look at him while she removed her life jacket.

Raoul would give it through tomorrow. After that, he'd do whatever it took to break her down, even talk to her mother.

Cami arrived at the villa at noon on Sunday looking gorgeous in a red sweater and black skirt. He'd left the back door open for her. Today she'd worn her hair tied back with a black-and-red print scarf. She was stunning. A flowery fragrance clung to her.

She was a vision, but Raoul didn't try to kiss her. "I hope you like steak for lunch." They were sizzling on the grill.

Cami flashed him one of those sunny smiles, but he knew she was hiding a secret from him. He had a hard time believing she hadn't recovered from her divorce. What else it could be he had no idea.

"First an Olympic swimming champion, now a *cordon bleu* chef!"

Laughter burst out of him. "Anything to impress you."

"Cam—" Alain called out pointing to her.

"Bonjour, Alain!" She hurried over to kiss him.

Raoul had put his son in the high chair

by the table and had wrapped a bib around his neck.

She sat down next to him. "Um. Junior chicken and noodles in the jar and a banana." Cami looked up at Raoul. "Can I feed him?"

"He's waiting for you."

He watched her get busy cutting the banana into bite-size pieces. "Do you want some bananas too?" she asked Raoul.

He chuckled and watched her find ingenious ways to feed him his chicken.

"Bana—"

"Yes. You want more of those, don't you?"

While she fed him, Raoul put the salad and brioches on the table with their plates of steak. Lunch was an incredibly happy affair. When it was time to leave, she wiped Alain's hands and mouth with a moist cloth.

"Lunch was delicious, Raoul. Thank you."

He had to get a grip on his emotions that were bursting inside of him. After finding his son's little coat, he put it on him and they walked out to the car. Alain was making happy noises as he fastened him in his car seat in back. Then he drove them down the drive to the main street. Cami talked to his son while Raoul took them to the estate and wound around to the cemetery.

The headstone for his grandfather hadn't been placed yet. Raoul kept going until he came to Jerome's grave and stopped the car.

"Will you come with us?"

"Of course."

She got out while he opened the back door and pulled Alain from his car seat. Holding him in one arm, he reached for the tin of flowers on the floor and carried everything to the site.

"Cam—" Alain called out and reached for her. To Raoul's delight she pulled him into her arms. He played with the ends of her scarf. Raoul put the daisies at the base of the monument.

"Aren't the flowers pretty?" She let Alain get down but held on to his hand. "Those are marguerites. Can you say *mar-guer-ites*?"

He listened, then said, *"Marg—"* emphasizing the hard *g*. It made her chuckle.

"That's right. Your papa sent my mother

marguerites. She loved them. I think they must be his favorite *fleur*."

"*Fleur.*"

"Yes!" Cami cried excitedly. "You know that word and are so smart." She leaned over to give him a hug. Though Raoul's thoughts were on Jerome, he watched her take Alain on a little walk, talking to him the whole time. Her tenderness with his son touched him to the core.

In a few minutes they walked back to the car and got settled. He turned to Cami. "Let's take him home and start a fire."

"I won't be able to stay. Maman and I have an early cleaning job." She was trying to act unaffected, but he saw the little nerve throbbing in her throat.

"How about my coming by for you tomorrow at five thirty? I won't press you about getting married, but I'd like an explanation of why you can't even talk about it. If you're no longer interested in me, I have to know the truth, whatever it is."

"I have a better idea. I'll come to the villa so you don't have to leave Alain. We can talk, but I won't be able to stay long."

"Thank you for that."

When they reached his house, she got out first. Maybe it was a trick of light, but he thought she'd lost some coloring. *"Au revoir, petit,"* she called out to Alain before shutting the door.

CHAPTER NINE

THIS AFTERNOON CAMI'S world had been completely transformed. She'd been with Raoul and Alain. It had felt like they were a family. He made her want things that were impossible, increasing her pain. She was in turmoil by the time she entered the apartment Sunday evening.

"There you are. I wondered when you'd get home."

"I went to the cemetery with Raoul and Alain. He wanted to put flowers on his great uncle's grave. I had the time of my life, and no, I still haven't told him about my heart condition. Please don't remind me it was a mistake."

"I wasn't going to say anything."

"I keep making them. Tomorrow I'm going to make one more and see him after work." He worried that she wasn't attracted to him anymore. If he only knew the truth.

All she could do was tell him she wasn't ready to talk about marriage. She had to be sure before she could make a commitment like that, and hoped he could deal with it. "But it will definitely be for the last time." At least until the operation was over and she knew anything concrete.

"Since you're getting so attached to the boy, it's probably better for him that you won't be there after tomorrow."

For him and for me.

Her mom knew she'd fallen fathoms deep in love with Raoul and his son, but she'd chosen the right words to bring her back to earth in a hurry.

"That's what I've been telling myself." Cami poured herself a drink of water. "How was your day?"

"We cleaned a house that had been damaged by a flood."

"We've done ones like that before. I hope it didn't hurt your shoulders too much."

"I'm fine. It's you I'm worried about. I'm not going to let you go to work on Tuesday. You need a day's rest before you go into the hospital."

Her love for Raoul wouldn't let her rest, but the surgery wouldn't be long now. Then what. *Oblivion?*

When Raoul saw Cami's car out in back, he got up from the table to open the back door for her. She'd come in jeans and a tan sweater, this time with her hair put back in a chignon. She was gorgeous no matter how she did it.

Alain called out to her from his high chair when she walked in the kitchen. Cami hurried over to the table and sat down by him.

"There's my boy," she said, giving him a kiss. "It looks like you've eaten all your dinner."

Just then an older woman came in the kitchen. She looked at Cami. "You must be *la fameuse Cam.*"

"Delphine LaVaux?" Raoul spoke up. "Let me introduce you to Cami Delon."

Cami chuckled, enjoying the woman's sense of humor. "It's very nice to meet you, Delphine. You have charge of a very precious little boy."

"You're right," the Parisian woman smiled. "We're slowly getting acquainted."

She liked the other woman on the spot.

"I've come in time to put you down for the night and read you a brand-new story I know you're going to like."

Raoul nodded. "He's all fed and ready."

Cami got up to undo the tray and pick him up. But when she went to hand Alain to the nanny, he let out a loud *"Non—Non—Cam—"* and hugged her around the neck.

Raoul came closer to intervene. He pulled his son out of Cami's arms and handed him to Delphine. "It's time for bed, *mon fils*."

"Come on, Alain," the older woman coaxed him. But he didn't like it and protested. Cami could hear him crying all the way through the house and up the stairs.

She glanced at Raoul. "Oh, dear."

"He'll get over it," Raoul reminded her. "These are early days."

"He's adorable."

"I'm biased and agree." He sat down. His penetrating black eyes studied her for a long moment. "You said you'd tell me the truth. I want to hear it."

Unbelievably his cell phone rang, interrupting them. This time he let out what sounded like a curse before he checked the caller ID. In an instant his brows furrowed and he clicked on, then jumped to his feet. After a short conversation, he hung up.

"That was Dominic. He says there's trouble at the winery and wants to pick me up. He swears it won't take long. I pray not because I need to talk to you before the night is out. Will you wait for me? Please?"

The urgency in his voice kept her planted there. "Of course. I hope it's not serious."

"You never know, but I'll be back as soon as I can." He raced through the villa and left out the front door.

A few minutes later the doorbell rang. Was it Raoul? Had he forgotten his key?

Cami hurried to the foyer. When she opened the door, she came face-to-face with a dark-haired attractive woman who had to be Raoul's mother. She was shorter than Cami would have supposed, but she and her son shared certain facial features around the nose and mouth you couldn't mistake.

Had she come because of the trouble and

wanted Raoul's help? She'd come with a package she held in her arm.

"May I help you? I'm Cami Delon."

"How do you do. I'm Madame Fontesquieu and I've come to see my son."

A second visitor. "I'm sorry, madame, but he isn't here. You just missed him. I don't believe he'll be long. Would you like to come in and wait for him?"

"I would. Thank you."

She'd dressed in a three-piece light green wool suit, the epitome of high fashion, and wore her hair in a becoming short style that revealed streaks of silver near the temples.

Cami showed her into the sitting room off the foyer. "May I bring you coffee while you wait?"

"That would be fine."

"I'll be right back." She hurried to the kitchen and poured her a cup, which she brought back to the sitting room. His mother was wandering around examining everything.

"Here you are."

The older woman turned around and sat down on the love seat to drink it. "Who are you exactly?"

"I'm a friend of Raoul's. We met while I was helping clean the villa. I work for Nettoyage Internationale here in Vence with my mother. We've been cleaning houses for seven years." His mother deserved to know the truth.

Her brown eyes narrowed on Cami. "Do you live here?"

That said it all. Raoul had warned her about the talk surrounding him. Sabine must have added her own assumption after coming to the villa. "*Non*, madame. I live with my mother."

"Who takes care of his son?"

So his mother *did* know about Alain. "His nanny, Delphine LaVaux."

"Is she here?"

"Yes."

"I would like to meet her."

"Excuse me. I'll go upstairs and tell her."

Cami hurried up to the next floor and found Delphine playing blocks with Alain in his bedroom. He called out her name when she walked in.

"*Bonsoir*, Alain." She gave him a peck on the cheek and looked at Delphine. "Excuse me, but Raoul's mother is here and wants to talk to you. She's in the sitting room, waiting."

The two women eyed each other before Delphine got up from the rocking chair and lifted Alain in her arms. "Come on, *mon petit.* Let's go see your *gran'mere*. It will be a first for both of us."

By that remark Cami deduced that Raoul had explained his family dynamics enough to Delphine that she understood certain facts. Cami could only admire her calm and maturity. She decided Raoul had hired an exceptional woman.

Delphine carried Alain downstairs. Cami followed. They found Raoul's mother on the phone. The minute they entered the sitting room, she put her cell phone in her purse and stood up.

Cami heard her sharp intake of breath as her brown eyes filled with tears the second they fastened on Alain. The likeness of him to her son had to have shocked the daylights out of her.

"Madame Fontesquieu, this is Delphine LaVaux."

"How do you do," Delphine spoke right up. "It's lovely to meet you, madame. You have a wonderful grandson. Come on, Alain." She tried to turn him so he'd look at Raoul's mother, but he fought her and kept his arms around her neck. "Say bonsoir to your *gran'mere*."

Alain started crying and wasn't having any of it.

"Let me take him in the kitchen for a snack," Delphine offered. "It will calm him down. We'll be right back."

Again Cami marveled over Delphine's handling of a very difficult situation. Her composure was worth its weight in gold and Raoul needed to know.

His mother reached for the package she'd put on an end table with the coffee cup and handed it to Cami. "Since you don't know how long he'll be gone, I've decided to leave. Please will you see that Raoul gets this?"

"*Très bien*, madame."

Cami followed her to the door and opened it for her. "He'll be sorry he missed you."

Her expression appeared haunted before she walked out on the porch and disappeared down the steps.

After closing it, she carried the package

to the kitchen. Delphine had put Alain in the high chair and was feeding him some strawberries.

"She's gone, Delphine."

"Raoul warned me his mother might come by one day. Can you imagine seeing your own grandchild for the first time? I think it went well enough. Who couldn't love this little angel?"

"Especially his *gran'mere.* He's absolutely angelic. Since it's getting late, I'm not sure when Raoul will be back. He had to leave on an emergency. I'll stay awhile longer, but then I must go. Please see that Raoul gets this package she brought him."

"Bien sûr."

"I'll go get the coffee cup left in the sitting room." Cami started through the house and walked right into Raoul's arms. He'd just come in and gripped her arms so she wouldn't fall.

"I'm so sorry," she blurted. "I didn't see you and now you've saved me from another fall."

"Where do you think you're going so fast?"

She eased away from his hard body. "I

need to get the coffee cup in the sitting room. Your mother came while you were gone. She brought you a gift. It's on the table in the kitchen."

Raoul hurried through the villa where he found Alain finishing off another strawberry. He kissed the top of his son's head. "Thank you for everything, Delphine. If you'll take him up to bed now, I need to talk to Cami."

"Of course."

"Bonne nuit, mon petit." He gave Alain another kiss before they left the kitchen.

Cami sank down on a chair while he opened the package.

"This is incredible," he murmured. "My mother has retrieved these without my having to resort to a court order to get them. I'm pleased beyond words."

"What are those?"

"The journals Jerome willed to me."

"Oh. That's wonderful!"

"Nothing could make me happier. I need them for the new business I've started. My mother knew how important they are to me and must have prevailed on Sabine to let me have them and the paintings."

"It sounds like your mother loves you very much."

"Mother hasn't known what to make of me for years."

"Why is that?"

"My father has never approved of my way of thinking about life and we've never seen eye to eye. Unfortunately he has intimidated her for years. I've rarely heard her express her true thoughts. She's afraid to say or do anything that will upset him. It took a great deal of daring for her to bring me those journals."

"But they belong to you!"

"True, but my father didn't want to lose Sabine. She fought the divorce, and held those journals and paintings back to use for leverage. My father loves the prestige of the Murat money and influence. He tried to make me hold on to Sabine at all costs. He even had my *gran'pere* declare me the CEO so I wouldn't divorce her. He held out against hope. That's the reason he refused to tell the truth to the media."

Finally Cami had the answer to that question. "According to the newscast, she brought millions to your marriage."

He nodded. “My father can’t bear to see me part with all her money. One day she’ll be an heiress. Her parents feel the same way about the Fontesquieu fortune. Being married to me, she had access to some of it.”

“Does your father know about Sabine’s lie to you?”

His dark head reared. “No one knows except Sabine, the doctor, Dominic and Nathalie, Arlette and now you.” And Cami’s mother. “That’s the way it’s going to stay. The ugliness over money and power in this family has gone on long enough. My father, along with Sabine and her parents, have done everything in their power to keep us together, but it’s far too late.”

“I love your mother for doing that for you.”

Their gazes met. “It’s a miracle she was able to convince Sabine to return the paintings and the journals to me. Naturally the news will get back to my father, and Maman will pay a price for it. That’s what concerns me.”

“It’s obvious she was willing to take the risk. That’s because you’re her only son and she has never stopped loving you. You have to know the truth of that deep down."

"I do. I think this was her way of giving me a peace offering. I told her recently that I would be leaving the business soon."

"I don't know how your father ever let you go."

"He had no choice."

"You know what I mean."

"I've told you about him. There's no hope where he's concerned. I've refused the CEO position. That, plus my divorce, has hardened his heart. When I said goodbye, he didn't try to stop me."

"How tragic for him, but I know your mother couldn't feel the same way. Oh, Raoul—you should have seen her eyes when she glimpsed Alain for the first time. They were flooded with tears. I had the distinct impression she was seeing you when you were his age. You both look so much alike."

"That's the reason Nathalie had such a hard time trying to figure out which Fontesquieu was Alain's father."

Cami smiled. "Delphine brought him downstairs and I introduced them to your mother who was speechless. I have to tell you that Delphine is the perfect person to be his nanny. She handled those first silent moments with your mother with such grace and respect, I was stunned."

"What about you? How did she treat you?"

"Your mother was civil."

Raoul stopped pacing. "That's what I was afraid of."

"Please don't misunderstand. The second she saw Alain, everything changed for her."

Raoul loved this woman who was trying her best to defend his mother. He moved closer. Using his free hand, he traced her beautiful features with his index finger. "Do you have any idea how wonderful you are?"

She averted her eyes. "Y-You're not listening to me," her voice faltered. "When I saw her to the door, I could tell she'd undergone a shock and I felt sorry for her. Alain is so adorable and she's missed out on the joy of watching her only grandson grow to this point. No doubt she has suffered over the loss of Celine, just as you have."

He loved the depths of this woman. "When I call to thank her for the gift, I'll tell her she can see him whenever she wants. We'll see if she can talk my father into coming around. But it's *you* I need to thank for being you and knowing how to deal with this whole ugly situation."

She was trembling. "Don't forget Delphine was a saint."

"In my opinion you're both candidates for the title. This news has made my day.

"Are you really all right, Raoul?"

He nodded. "The trouble at the winery was easily solved. Word still hasn't reached some of the workers that I'm no longer associated with the business. They insisted on an explanation."

"It's hard for people to let go."

"That's true for me too. What is the one thing you haven't told me? I'm still waiting for that answer."

"I'll give you one, but I didn't expect to stay this long."

"That's my fault."

"I promise we'll talk again, but not tonight. Suffice it to say I'm not ready to talk about marriage yet. It's too soon."

"So are you saying you need more time?"

"Yes, now I have to go." She got up from the table.

"Cami—"

"Please—it's all I can tell you right now."

It was pure torture to watch her leave. He waited until he saw her headlights and she'd gone. If she needed time, he'd give it to her.

The first thing he did after getting in bed later was phone his mother. Cami's explanation over what had happened earlier went a long way to help him find the right words.

"Maman?"

"Raoul… Thank heaven you called."

There was new warmth in her voice. "As if I wouldn't. I'd planned to invite you over next week to meet Alain."

"I…decided I didn't want to wait. He's wonderful and looks so much like you, I—I couldn't believe it," her voice faltered.

"So are you for coming on your own and bringing the journals. How did you manage it?"

"I reminded Sabine that those were your private possessions and she had no right to them. She hasn't been kind about a lot of things for a long time. She was especially negative about Camille Delon. I'm afraid I wasn't friendly to her when she answered the door. She said she was a friend and that she'd helped clean your house."

"Maman, Camille Delon is the love of my life and the woman I'm going to marry," Raoul declared. It was a relief to say it out loud.

"Married? I guess that doesn't surprise me. I'm very much aware you love that little boy's mother and no one else. How soon are you planning the wedding?"

"I hope to have that answer soon, but I need to tell you the truth of things. Cami's not his mother."

"What do you mean?"

"Alain's birth mother died ten days after he was born."

The silence was deafening. "She's dead?"

"That's right. Over eighteen months ago. Her name was Antoinette Fournier. She's buried in La Gaude. I'd planned to marry her. Instead I had to give her up. Her wonderful mother, Arlette, and her stepsister, Nathalie, raised him until a few months ago when Nathalie traced him to me."

"Dominic's wife?" Too many shocks in one day, but his mother needed to know the truth. Of necessity there'd been too much secrecy.

"Yes. She was looking for me when she met Dominic and they fell in love. She is Alain's adored aunt. Now I'd like him to get to know and love you. You're his *gran'mere*. I've already told his nanny that you don't need an invitation to know you're welcome at the villa anytime. Cami knows it too."

"When did you meet Cami?"

"The day after *gran'pere* passed away."

"And you're in love this fast?"

"Madly, desperately. I didn't think it could happen again in this life, but it did and I wanted you to know before anyone else." He told her about Cami's story and her trips to the vineyard with her father and mother. "She used to dream she was the princess in the château."

"She sounds very sweet and was very polite to me. Why don't you plan to marry her in the château chapel? It would thrill me to know you're going to marry the woman of your heart there, even if you have moved out."

Raoul couldn't believe what he was hearing. "What about Papa?"

"Leave him to me. He's suffering over you. A marriage at the château might be just what he needs to feel better about everything."

That had to be a first. "I'll think about it."

"I can see there's a lot we have to discuss. *Je t'aime, mon fils*," her voice trembled. "I'll visit soon to get acquainted with her and my grandson."

Those were brave words considering she had to deal with his father. "Can you come over tomorrow? No one else will be around. Alain will love it."

"I'll work something out and let you know."

His throat swelled with emotion. "*Je t'aime*, Maman."

Raoul couldn't sleep all night and finally got up to shower and shave. At seven the next morning he hurried to the nursery. Alain was standing up in his crib waiting for him. The sight thrilled him every time. He put him in some rompers and carried him down to the kitchen where they both ate breakfast.

Cami had gone home last night and there'd been nothing he could do about it. The second Alain had discovered she'd gone, he'd started to cry. It had taken Raoul quite a while to console him before he fell asleep in his crib.

If his mother could come over later, she'd phone him first, but he worried his father might have other plans. Raoul decided to take Alain to Arlette's for the day. He needed to have that serious talk with Cami, and didn't believe she wasn't ready for marriage. She was holding a secret he needed to get out of her.

A part of him had hoped she might try to reach him last night, but it hadn't happened. All morning he waited for a phone call, then he phoned her. To his chagrin, the call went through to her voice mail. Worse, he couldn't leave a message because the box was full.

He hung up in frustration. Toward the end of the day he walked into the kitchen where Arlette was feeding Alain. "I'm leaving for a while, but I'll stay in touch with you."

"Go for as long as you want, or overnight. We'll have great fun here, won't we, Alain?"

"Thanks, Arlette. I couldn't do without you."

Raoul kissed his son and left the house. He assumed Cami and her mom were at the apartment in Vence and had decided not to take calls. They'd be home from work by now. He would drive by to see if their Citroën 2CV was parked there. If so, he'd knock on the door and surprise her.

A half hour later more disappointment met him when there was no sign of the black car around the eight-plex. Still, he got out and knocked on their door in case one of them was home. When that didn't work, he walked to the next apartment and knocked, hoping to get some information. Unfortunately no one was home there either.

As a last resort, he went back to his car and called NI. He had to leave a message and asked the manager to phone him back ASAP.

Madame Biel called him ten minutes later.

"Monsieur Fontesquieu? I just saw the message that you'd phoned in. I have found a woman whom I believe would make an excellent housekeeper. Her name is Charisse Verot. Shall I make an appointment for her to come to the villa?"

That had been the last thing on his mind, but he might as well deal with it now. "Could she come next Monday? Say 10:00 a.m.?"

"She'll be there."

"Thank you, but before we hang up, I need to ask you a question. Did the Delon family work today?"

"Actually no. They've gone on vacation."

A day earlier than planned? "Do you have Juliette's phone number?"

"Of course. Here it is."

Raoul put it in his phone. "I'd like to get in touch with her and find out what their plans might be. I've tried phoning Camille several times, but her voice mail is full."

"I'm sorry about that, monsieur. They didn't share any of their plans with me."

"I understand. Thank you for returning my call."

"Of course. I hope Madame Verot works out well for you."

"We'll see."

Right now he couldn't concentrate on anything. At this point Raoul was convinced that Cami was deliberately hiding from him. He phoned both numbers. Even Juliette's message box was full.

Grimacing, Raoul went back to his villa and spent the night. In the morning he drove to a café for a quick breakfast and went back to the Delon apartment once more. By now he knew in his gut something was terribly wrong.

Their black car still wasn't there, but that didn't matter. He pulled into the parking area at the side of the building and got out to investigate. There was no answer after he knocked and rang the doorbell. For the next little while he knocked on the other apartment doors of the eight-plex to see if anyone was home and knew anything about the Delon family.

Unbelievably no one answered. He went back to the car and sat there to wait. Someone had to come home eventually. He'd stay there all day if he had to and phoned Dominic to tell him what was going on.

"I know she's avoiding me, Dom."

"Then stick to your plan and find out what you can from the neighbors. If you need more help, I'll be available after work to help."

"No one ever had a better friend."

They hung up. Around four thirty a woman probably close to Juliette's age, pulled into the parking and got out.

Raoul called to her from his car window so he wouldn't alarm her. "Excuse me, madame. Do you live here? I'm looking for Cami and Juliette Delon. Do you know them?"

The woman smiled. "Yes. They live in the apartment next to mine."

His heart pounded fiercely. Maybe this waiting had produced results after all. "My name is Raoul Fontesquieu. I've been trying to reach Cami. She and her mother were on the team that cleaned my villa two weeks ago."

"I remember Juliette telling me they had a big job. You're the one who sent the flowers!"

"That's right."

"How can I help you?"

"Did you see either of them today?" She shook her head. "Do you know their plans now that they're on vacation?"

"I believe they were intending to be with family in Nice like they always do."

Nice? Cami had never mentioned extended family living there. Why had she lied to him that she wouldn't be leaving Vence? What kind of a secret had she been keeping from him? "Do you have a name or an address where I can contact her there?"

"I'm sorry. All I know is they always spend time with her father's family."

Her *father's* family with a last name *Delon*? "Thank you. You've been very helpful."

After she walked off, he phoned Delphine and told her he might not be home all night. She assured him she could stay indefinitely.

With that resolved, he drove to the office on the estate to see Dominic and eat dinner with him. Between the two of them they could get on the phone and try to track down Cami's family.

CHAPTER TEN

CAMI'S MOTHER DECIDED to go on vacation a day early. They left town on Monday and drove to Nice with their suitcases. They spent the next two nights there with family and got everything ready so that when they returned after the operation, they'd have what they needed.

Those were difficult nights to get through for Cami. On Wednesday they drove back to Vence and checked into the hospital. That evening the technician doing Cami's labs had finished drawing blood for a second time. After he left the hospital room, housekeeping came in and set up a cot where her mother would sleep for the night.

Now that they were alone, Cami eyed her ever faithful mom who stood at the side of her bed.

"Well, Maman, this is it. By tomorrow

morning at nine o'clock, Dr. Molette explained that the keyhole surgery will be over."

"That's right. He said you would have smaller scars and get out of the hospital quicker. Better yet you'll have less pain while the scars heal and will get back to normal activities sooner."

"That's an impossible dream, Maman."

"Nothing's impossible, Cami."

She sat up straighter in the bed. "You also heard him say that if it doesn't work, I'll have to come in again for open-heart surgery after he returns from vacation."

Her mom reached for her hand. "It'll be a success. Your uncle Emil and aunt Liliane have planned for us to come to their house while you recover. Everyone is anxious to wait on you."

Cami loved her father's older brother and his wife. He ran a small trucking company in Nice. They lived in a charming home where she'd spent many hours over the years, especially during the semesters while she'd been attending the university.

"That would be wonderful, but I don't have your faith about the outcome of the operation. We might not be going anywhere."

I might not make it out of the hospital.

"Nonsense. You've always been so brave about this, and I'm so happy it's finally here I could cry."

"You and me both."

"It hasn't been fair to you all these years, waiting and waiting."

Cami squeezed her mom's fingers gently. "Nor to you. Have I told you how much I love you? When I was with Raoul on his sailboat, he told me a story about his tragic relationship with his father. It made me appreciate even more being born to the best parents in the world."

Her mom's eyes watered. "Thank you, darling. Certainly you know how much joy you bring to mine. But let's change the subject because I know how deeply in love you are with Raoul. Why not tell me what else happened while you were out there with him?"

"H-He wanted me to go to a party at his cousin's place in a couple of weeks." She stumbled over her words. "But I told him I'd be on vacation. After we got back to the villa, I thanked him for a lovely time, said goodbye and left."

"And he let you go, just like that?" Her mom was going to keep this up until she'd wrung the truth from her.

Cami hugged the pillow against her. "No," came her muffled response, but the tears falling down her cheeks betrayed her. "He asked me to marry him."

"That doesn't surprise me a bit, but you obviously said no or he'd be here at your side this very minute."

"I couldn't put him through this."

"Why not?"

"Because I haven't told you everything about his life. While he was married, his wife had a baby girl."

"He had a baby with his wife?"

Cami stared at her mom. "But he found after the birth that his little daughter, Celine, wasn't *his*!"

A frown broke out on her mother's face. "His wife *lied* to him about that?"

Cami nodded. "She tricked him so he would marry her."

"Ah. That explains why he had to let

Alain's mother go and he never got to see his own boy."

"There's more, Maman. He adored that baby in spite of the lie, but suffered grief when the doctor told them the little girl had such a damaged heart, she wouldn't survive. They buried her on the Fontesquieu estate a month after she was born."

Cami watched her mother pace for a moment before she came to a halt. "I finally have my answer why you never told him about tomorrow's surgery."

"How could I after all he's been through? He loved that baby and it killed him she died of a bad heart!" Cami cried. At this point she broke down sobbing. "He's so remarkable, so wonderful and doesn't deserve to go through any more pain or suffering."

"That's because you're convinced that you're not going to make it."

"I don't know what to believe," she bit out. "Can you guarantee I *won't* die?"

Silence reigned for a moment. "No, my darling girl, but I know God is watching over you and He's not going to let that happen. Excuse me while I freshen up in your bathroom, then I'll come in and lie down on that cot by you. I want to hear more about this incredible man who's going to become my son-in-law one day."

"Don't joke with me about this."

"Who's joking?" she asked from the bathroom door.

"I'm afraid you're not going to get much sleep." Cami wiped her eyes. "The nurse will be in and out during the night."

"It'll be worth it when morning comes and I find out my daughter came through her surgery perfectly and will be free of worry for the rest of her life about her heart."

Free of worry.

Incredibly, for the first time in years, Cami had something else on her mind besides the outcome of the surgery. She was still so shaken by the feel of being in Raoul's arms, let alone his marriage proposal, she couldn't think straight.

Raoul had been right about one thing. She'd fallen crazy in love with him and his son. The way she'd returned his soul-searching kisses told him everything she hadn't been able to say in words.

Cami had escaped his world just in time. He deserved to find a woman of his own class who would love Alain and make a wonderful home for him. She would have to be a woman of whom his parents could approve of. Cami didn't care how much Raoul denied it, his father's opinion had to mean something to him. She could never be his parent's choice of daughter-in-law.

Of course, Cami's mother didn't have the same problem when it came to Raoul. She'd approved of him from the beginning.

But the only matter of importance was tomorrow, the most important day of her life. Until the operation was over, she had no idea what her life would be like. No one could predict the future.

Antoinette had died of infection ten days after giving birth to Alain. Within a month of being born, Sabine's baby had died of a bad heart, adding to Raoul's grief over the lie she'd told him.

Maybe Cami wouldn't come out of the anesthetic. Thank heaven her mother had family to turn to if the worst happened and Cami's heart stopped beating altogether.

Anything could happen. Thankfully her beloved Raoul would know nothing about it. That was the way it had to be.

The next morning, her operation was scheduled early. Before going to sleep the night before, they'd given her a medication to make her less anxious. When morning came she was administered the anesthetic. When Cami awakened in the recovery room later on, she saw her doctor smiling at her.

"Welcome to the world, Cami. Your mother told me how frightened you've been, but you don't have to be any longer. Your operation was a complete success. You're going to live a long, full life. For now you must rest. You'll be taken to your room in a little while. Tomorrow I'll release you."

Cami couldn't believe it. Tears spurted from her eyes. "You mean I'm not dreaming? I'm really going to have a normal life?"

"Yes." He patted her arm. "I understand there's a wonderful man out there somewhere who'll rejoice when he hears this news. But for the time being you need to stay quiet and rest."

Raoul.

More tears streamed from her eyes. She was alive! The operation was over and she was going to live a full life. She couldn't wait to tell Raoul everything!

Two days later Cami and her mom drove to Nice to be with the family while she recovered. Cami half lay on the bed in her robe watching the 5:00 p.m. news, but one announcement caused her to sit up straight.

"More news from Provence. Matthieu Fontesquieu has been named CEO of the Fontesquieu empire in Vence due to his son, Raoul Fontesquieu, stepping down after his divorce from Sabine Murat. More on this story is forthcoming."

"Raoul, darling," she whispered to herself. His father had finally accepted what had happened. Now Raoul had gotten his wish and was now truly on his own.

She gotten her wish too.

The operation had made her well! Joy, joy! Since the doctor had talked to her in the recovery room, she'd wanted to phone Raoul and tell him everything, but had needed to wait a few days until her strength had returned.

Her mom had gone to the beauty parlor to get her hair done and hadn't returned yet.

That's what Cami needed to do. Hers needed to be cut. It had grown too long to manage.

"Cami?"

"Come in."

Her sandy-haired aunt Liliane peeked inside. "I have a message for you from Emil."

She couldn't imagine. "What is it?" They'd been so wonderful to her.

"Raoul Fontesquieu would like you to call him as soon as you can. Apparently your message box is full and he hasn't been able to get through. Emil said he sounded pretty desperate on the phone."

"Raoul talked to Emil? But how could he?"

"I don't know." Her aunt smiled.

"No one knows where I've been recuperating!"

"Why don't you call him and find out?"

Cami couldn't believe it. No one at NI, or at the hospital had any idea where she'd been. Had he hired someone to find her? Would he actually do that? This wasn't supposed to have happened. She'd planned to call him tomorrow.

Too many emotions had converged at once, but the one that overpowered her most was a joy beyond bearing. According to the doctor, the keyhole surgery had fixed her heart. She wouldn't have to worry about it ever again. But right this second it was beating so hard, she feared there could be real damage.

Her aunt was still standing there. "Did he tell Raoul I've had heart surgery?"

"No. He feels it's your place to do that."

"Tell him thank you for that. I promise to get hold of Raoul tomorrow."

"I think that would be a good idea."

From that point on Cami was an excited, nervous wreck. She kept going through her mind how she would approach him and what she would say. Finally she got on her laptop and sent an email to the Degardelle Company.

Dear Sir

My name is Edouard Sorel. I'm from Marseilles and read your ad in La Provence. I've been in Nice and would like to meet you in person.

I realize it's quick notice, but I'm afraid to get into something and fill out forms without meeting the head man first.

Would it be possible to come to your office in Vence? I only have a small amount of money to purchase land for a future vineyard and have several spots in mind. Perhaps none of them will do, but I'd like to hear what an expert like you has to say.

I could be there by tomorrow evening at seven if that works for you. Otherwise I'll have to wait a month before I can come back to Vence.

I await your response.

Sick with nerves and excitement over what she'd done, she hurried to the salon to tell the family her plans. They all had dinner, then she hurried back to the bedroom to see if he'd answered. She trembled with happiness to read his response.

Monsieur Sorel.

I'll meet you at seven.

I'm afraid it will have to be a short meeting because I have another engagement.

Just follow the map and knock at the outside door with the sign on it.

Cami answered.

Merci mille fois, monsieur. I'll be there on time.

She closed the lid of the laptop. "Raoul Fontesquieu? Get ready for a big surprise, my love."

The next day Cami and her mom drove back to their apartment in Vence. The doctor cautioned her to be careful. She had to take it easy, but it was good for her to be up and around. Depending on how things went, her mom might return to Nice the next day. As for Cami, anything could happen.

She took a shower and washed her hair. This time she would wear it long again and brushed it from a side part until it gleamed. The last time they'd been together, he'd revealed how much he loved it loose.

She pulled her dressiest dress out of the closet. A sleeveless, filmy black affair with a round neck. Cami had only worn it one time to a party with her friends after they'd graduated in November. The operation had transformed her into a new woman.

After putting on her lavender-blue earrings and slipping on her black high-heeled sandals, she was ready. It was time to knock the socks off her prince. Before leaving the apartment, she changed handbags to the silky black one. Then she gathered the shopping bag holding some gifts for him and Alain.

One more item to go. A stylish, waist-length black coat she'd spent some money on when she'd bought the dress. Cami was so glad she'd purchased it. There'd be no sign of the cleaning lady tonight.

Giving her mother a kiss, she left the apartment and got in the car. Despite the fact that she was still recuperating from the operation, her body was so alive, she could be a rocket getting ready to fly into space.

Raoul kissed his son who was still in his high chair. "Be good for Delphine." He eyed the nanny who was turning out to be a treasure. She'd had a lot to put up with since he'd returned from Nice so devastated he was barely functioning. So far no return call from Cami. "I'll look in on him later. I have a client coming to the office."

"This late?"

"It's all right. What else do I have to do but try to make more money?" He heard her chuckle before he left the kitchen and went upstairs to shower and shave. In a few minutes he put on dark trousers and a dark blue long-sleeved sport shirt. When he was ready, he headed for his office.

Dominic's brother Etienne had invited him over to the château for dinner. He loved him, but didn't want to go near the place. They settled on meeting at Le Petit Auberge at nine.

As soon as he entered his office, he heard the knock on the door. He walked over, but when he opened it, he was surprised to smell the delicious flower fragrance Cami wore.

"*Bonsoir*, Monsieur Fontesquieu." When she walked in looking a heavenly vision in black, he thought he was hallucinating.

"*Cami—*"

"I'm afraid Monsieur Sorel couldn't make it because he doesn't exist. I made him up and hope you're not angry with me. The thing is, I had to see you or die in the attempt. I can't live without you, Raoul. That's why I'm here." Her eyes dazzled like rare amethysts. "I love you more than life itself, but you better not touch me until I can explain."

"What do you mean?"

"I'm recovering from a heart operation I underwent on the eighteenth."

"A heart operation?" He looked staggered by the information.

"I know it's a shock for you to hear that. Like your Celine, I was born with a heart murmur, but by some miracle the surgeon was able to fix it. In another two weeks I'll have recovered enough to get back to normal living. I'm afraid for you to hold me too tightly."

One look at Raoul's chiseled features while he stood there with a more princely aura than any royal and Cami almost passed out. His blazing black eyes played over every inch of her, missing absolutely nothing. The intensity of his gaze robbed her of breath. She walked to the love seat and sat down so she wouldn't sink to the floor.

"Are you still in a lot of pain?"

"No. The cuts are healing and I no longer have to take painkillers."

"Dieu merci," Raoul muttered.

"I've been waiting five years for the keyhole surgery to be performed. It's a good thing I did because the new technology fixed everything."

His eyes moistened. "When I think of all your hard work, I—"

"My heart condition didn't stop me from doing normal activity," she broke in on him. "I was glad for all the tasks. They helped me from thinking too much."

"But if I'd known the trial you were facing, I would have come to the hospital and stayed with you. I can't believe you went through that experience without me."

"Raoul, you've gone through enough suffering, especially over Celine. I didn't want to add to it until I knew the outcome."

He closed his eyes for a moment. "You've been a hard person to find," he spoke in his deep voice that set every cell of her body on fire. "I tried to call, but your message box has been full."

She swallowed hard. "I know. I left it that way on purpose. How did you know where to find me?"

"Your next-door neighbor at the apartment."

"I don't understand. She wouldn't have known anything."

"When I asked her if she knew your plans, she said you always went on vacation with your father's family in Nice. It only took me and Dominic six hours to eliminate every Delon who lives there until I found your uncle Emil at his trucking company.

"When I explained I needed to talk to you, he phoned your aunt. But he didn't tell me about your heart."

"I didn't want you to know about it until I could tell you in person. But I wasn't sure I'd be able to tell you anything if I didn't make it out of the operating room. I had fears about dying. That probably sounds hysterical to you."

"No it doesn't. What hurts me is that you've kept all those fears to yourself." He sounded more emotionally upset than she'd ever heard him.

"You didn't need to hear about my condition, which would be a reminder of all you've suffered. When I told you about my bad marriage, I never told you that my ex couldn't cope with my condition. He freaked out when I told him I couldn't run in a marathon he wanted to do. I guess he thought I might die. I don't know what he thought. He wouldn't talk to me about it."

"So you thought I wouldn't be able to handle it either."

"I didn't know, darling."

He raked a hand through his black hair in what she knew reflected pain and frustration. "You remained silent for *my* sake."

"Because I loved you so much."

"Thank heaven you came into my life. We felt an instant attraction and were thrown together long enough to realize we want to spend the rest of our lives together.

"Now that you've been told you'll never have heart trouble again, there's nothing to stop us from being together forever. Let's get married before you have to start work. I've already talked to my mother about it. She wants us to get married in the chapel at the château. She was very impressed with you and wants us to be happy."

Cami was overcome. "She really wants us to be married at your old home?"

"Yes. She thinks it might even soften my father."

"Is that what you would want?"

"I can't think of anything more wonderful than marrying my long-haired princess in the château she loved as a child."

"With Alain as our witness?" she cried with happiness."

"Absolutely."

"What's he going to say when he grows older and finds out I was your cleaning lady?"

"By that time he'll discover his brilliant mother is a Renaissance woman who's part of the vital financial team at Gaillard's."

"Now I know I'm dreaming. Oh, Raoul—" Cami's throat swelled. "I want so much to be the perfect wife and mother."

"My mother already likes you."

"Mine adores you. She's not going to believe it when I tell her where we're going to be married."

"Maman is sorry she wasn't kinder to you that day and is looking forward to getting to know you."

"Thank you for telling me that. I want so much to be the perfect mother and wife. But I know your father won't be happy."

"Not at first, but hopefully in time he'll come around. Just remember that part of life is getting hurt and we'll deal with it if and when it happens."

He reached out and drew her into his arms. "You and I have both found that out in the past. But instead of dwelling on the dark side of everything, why don't you start chasing after the sunshine? I think my fortune cookie was meant for you," he whispered against her lips.

"Raoul."

"*Mon amour.* It's been too long. Kiss me so I can believe you're back in my arms, alive and well." He ran his fingers through her shoulder-length hair. "You don't know long I've wanted to do this. You're so breathtaking I'm never going to be the same again."

Raoul clasped her gently, but her shopping bag and purse fell to the floor. "I can't believe it's you. You're the most beautiful sight this man has ever seen," he cried before covering her mouth with his own. In a heartbeat they were devouring each other.

When he couldn't get close enough, he removed her coat, then carried her back to the love seat and caught her against him. They clung, trying to show each other how they felt. "I love you so desperately, Cami."

She kissed every inch of his face. "I

wanted to come the day I woke up in recovery, but had to wait a few days."

"If you only knew what I've been through since you said goodbye to me."

"I'm so sorry, darling." Tears poured down her flushed cheeks. "You know I didn't mean it. In the beginning I was just so afraid I couldn't be the wife you wanted, or the mother Alain needs. I was afraid to let things go further, but somehow they did."

Raoul groaned. "You think I don't know that?" He started kissing her again until neither of them could stop. "Are you ready to marry me now?"

"You know I am or I wouldn't be here. The doctor told me I could get back to real normal in another two weeks."

"Then that settles it. Stay right there. I've got something for you." He kissed her long and hard before hurrying over to his desk. After reaching for something inside the top drawer, he rushed back to her and got down on one knee.

"Camille Delon, will you do me the honor of marrying me?"

"Oh, Raoul, yes!" she cried. More tears

ran from her eyes. He caught hold of her left hand and pushed a gold ring with a large violet-blue stone onto her ring finger.

"You've just made me the happiest man alive." He pulled her down gently and they ended up entwined on the floor. "I love you, I love you."

"Darling—"

The world reeled away as they got lost in each other's arms. So deep was their rapture, Raoul didn't realize there was a knock on the door.

"What is it, Delphine?"

"Your son wants to say good night."

"Come in."

She opened the door. Alain stood there clinging to her hand. Raoul didn't know which of the four of them was the most surprised.

"Cam!" It took his son a few seconds to recognize her with flowing hair.

Cami sat up looking gloriously disheveled and held out her arms. He came running into them. "Oh, my darling, darling boy. You really are going to be *my* boy!"

Raoul looked up at Delphine with moist eyes. She stood in the entry. He got to his feet. "You're the first to know that Cami and I are getting married."

The nanny was all smiles. "I've been hoping for this. Congratulations. Unless you need me, I'll be upstairs."

"Thank you, Delphine." He turned to Cami. She was entertaining Alain. He watched her hand him a present from the shopping bag lying on the floor.

Alain tore at the wrapping and unveiled a red toy Jaguar that looked just like Raoul's car. He couldn't believe it. Suddenly she looked up at him and handed him a package. "This is for you, *mon amour*."

In a daze, Raoul took it from her. After undoing the wrapping, he came face-to-face with an eight-by-ten framed photograph of a young, handsome Jerome. "Where in heaven's name did you find this? I've never seen this one." Raoul was stunned.

"I searched the internet and found a story about him when he lived in Bordeaux. There was an article about the vineyard and pictures. This one brought him to life for me. He loved you so much and it spoke to my heart. I forwarded it to a shop that made up this picture for me. They're doing another one of Danie I'll pick up in a few days."

Raoul got back on the floor where his son was moving the car around. He reached for Cami and pulled her down to him. "You couldn't have given me anything I'd treasure more. I'm so in love with you I think I'm the one with the heart condition now."

They began kissing again, but his phone rang. He ignored it the first time, but when the caller didn't give up, he let her go long enough to pull the cell out of his pocket.

"*Zut.* It's Etienne. I agreed to meet him for dinner at nine."

She grinned. "It's kind of late, like ten o'clock. Why don't you call him back and invite him to come over. In fact why don't you invite Dominic and Nathalie too. I'd like to meet them all."

"You mean it?" He was on the verge of exploding from joy.

"*Bien sûr, mon cheri.* It's going to be so exciting for me to have cousins. We can announce our engagement to them. Alain will love having everyone here. I'll go out to the kitchen and cook up some appetizers. I know you have a stock of your best wine in the cupboard. We'll party for as long as we want. What do you say?"

"I say I've died and gone to heaven with the two people I love most in this world."

"That's exactly how I feel. But I'd like to stay on the earth long enough to have your baby. Alain is going to need a brother or sister."

"Speaking of brother or sister, Dom and Nathalie just found out they're expecting."

"That's fantastic."

"Like I said, we need to get married immediately. Dominic knows a judge who'll waive all the rules for us."

"I have to admit I don't mind marrying into your aristocratic family after all. A perk like that I can live with. But the greatest one of all is that I'm actually going to marry the prince I once dreamed about. Dreams like that just don't come true in real life."

"Kiss me again before I call my cousins. They'll be in shock when they find out I'm marrying the most gorgeous woman in all Provence."

Alain came running over and clasped them both around the legs. He looked up with those shiny black eyes so much like Raoul's, Cami melted.

"Papa—Cam—"

"Oh, darling—" Her heart was bursting with happiness.

Raoul pulled her closer. "This is heaven."

* * * * *

If you missed the previous story in
Escape to Provence duet,
check out

Falling for Her French Tycoon

And if you enjoyed this story,
look out for these other great reads from
Rebecca Winters

How to Propose to a Princess
The Prince's Forbidden Bride
The Princess's New Year Wedding

All available now!